THE CLIFF LINE

THE CLIFF LINE

M. Wiseman

Copyright © 2009 by Israel Bookshop Publications

ISBN 978-1-60091-094-4

All rights reserved. No part of this book may be reproduced or transmitted in any form or by any means (electronic, photocopying, recording or otherwise) without prior permission of the publisher.

The Cliff Line is a work of fiction, based only on imagination and not on real people or places. Any resemblances are purely coincidental.

For constructive criticism, comments, or suggestions, the author can be contacted at: mattiewiseman@yahoo.com.

Book and cover design by Zippy Thumim

Published by:
Israel Bookshop Publications
501 Prospect Street
Lakewood, NJ 08701
Tel: (732) 901-3009
Fax: (732) 901-4012

www.israelbookshoppublications.com
info@israelbookshoppublications.com

Printed in Canada

To my parents,
Mr. Shmuel and Mrs.
Golda Wiseman

To my older brother,
Nochum, and my
younger siblings, Mindi,
Shoshana, Elchonon,
Chaim Tzvi, and
Dovid Yehudah

TABLE OF CONTENTS

Prologue 1
Chapter 1 — Why Ben Loves His Job 3
Chapter 2 — Kehillath Rabbi Norton 15
Chapter 3 — Dinner Time 23
Chapter 4 — What a Wonderful Day 33
Chapter 5 — Sparks 43
Chapter 6 — Spelt Challos 51
Chapter 7 — Shabbos 63
Chapter 8 — Unexpected Guests 77
Chapter 9 — So Long and Hello 93
Chapter 10 — Slight Chance of Showers 101
Chapter 11 — Rainfall 127
Chapter 12 — The Plot Thickens 159
Chapter 13 — Reckonings 167
Chapter 14 — No Fairytale Ending 185
Chapter 15 — So Long and Farewell 201
Epilogue 209
Acknowledgements /About the Author 219

PROLOGUE

The scent of ancient *sefarim*....so holy, so beautiful, so inviting. The *kedushah* clings to the pages and surrounds the learner in an almost hypnotic calmness. The words draw one forward to the meaning, each verse tugging and smoothing the ragged edges of a mind so troubled by the world around it. To toil in its seas, to struggle and compare, to take what has been written and draw yourself into it. Proving, disproving, concentrating one's strength to pinpoint an idea, and then pulling others to it.

Torah.

What is Torah?

Torah is water.

Torah is life.

When the rush of the day is over, Rabbi Norton can be found in his study. It is a place for him to detoxify and recharge his *geshmak*. Four walls lined with tomes of every size and color, with a step-stool waiting patiently in the corner to support his short, portly stature.

He carefully places his cup of coffee on the edge of the teetering table and eases himself into his armchair. His gaze passes over the stack of gemaras in a corner of the table, lingering, wanting. Then, with a sigh, he tugs at his beard. He reaches for the stack of mail in his overflowing in-box.

Bills, bills, more bills. *Nu*, the price of running such a beautiful community and such a wonderful family. If only the rest of the world would be *zocheh* to have such problems. Ha, if only the rest of the world would be *zocheh* to pay these bills.

The *goyishe* Rosh Hashanah brought on a *teshuvah* of some sort with a *frei* Yid named Dr. Rosen, and now January is well paid for. "*Tizku l'mitzvos*, Dr. Rosen," thinks Rabbi Norton.

Now, for his home. The utility bill must be paid, but maybe the orthodontist can be paid in installments? Wait...what's this? An envelope, thick and cream-colored. Morgan Towers? Rob... Does he know a Rob? There's no last name, no anything, as if this fellow Rob expected that Rabbi Norton should automatically know him.

The letter reads: *I hope all is well with you. However, I thought I should inform you that your dealings with my nephew are illegal. I would like to politely advise you to discontinue any interaction as soon as possible. Sincerely, Rob.*

A nephew? And does this fellow say who this nephew is and what the problem is....? *Nu*, there are plenty of *meshuganehs* around in this world. *Nebbach*, who knows what the story is with this one? With a shrug, Rabbi Norton crumples the letter and tosses it into the wastebasket.

CHAPTER 1
WHY BEN LOVES HIS JOB

On the corner of 17th and B there stands a tower of steel and glass. It rises forty floors into the air before the sides narrow to meet at a point twenty floors further. This being a city quite set upon by pigeons, one cannot help but pity the window-washer.

This is Morgan Tower, the place Ben leaves the comforting warmth of his bed for at the unearthly hour of nine each morning.

Today, as all days, Ben enters the lobby and stands at the 'v-lator,' clicking the button again and again, for it is a known fact that the more you press a button, the faster the results.

Ben is running late.

People do not run late in Morgan Enterprises.

And so the 'v-lator' naturally takes its time arriving.

Then, with a "whoosh," the capsule is sucked into place and the door opens, beckoning Ben in, as if to say: "Oh, Ben, are you late? That's too bad. I was just too busy counting ceiling tiles to come any sooner."

Ben enters in quick bounds. "Fifty-ninth floor," he says in a snappish tone. He leaves his stomach behind as he shoots up. Within seconds, the door flaps open once more, to place him before another door, steel-bound and cold.

"Name, please," says a voice, all sweetly telemarketer-lady-crisp.

"Ben Burns."

A blue laser light comes from nowhere, and he tries not to blink as it scans his eyes. Fans suck in the particles they blow off his clothing, checking for lethal materials.

Finally, the steel door opens and he exits the 'v-lator' into a hallway of dingy lights and restaurant-like black and white tiles.

The ceiling is low and the walls are cracked. The baseboard is covered in dust and paint chips litter the floor. Somewhere far off, a tap drip-drips. Ben shakes his head irritably, then makes for his office straight down to the right — #5908.

He stops at the door and fumbles with the key chain on his belt loop, pawing desperately through the keys.

Gold and silver. Square and circle. Big and small. No office key.

Where's that blasted thing when you need it? Oh, of course it would be the very last key on the chain. He jabs it haphazardly in the general direction of the key hole, managing by some luck to eventually slip it in. He twists it with a rapid flick of his wrist and enters, letting the door swing shut behind him.

The room flares green before fading into a comfortable yellow.

"Mr. Burns — *has arrived*," a voice announces. "Time. — *9:34*. You are — *late*."

"Ya, ya," he mutters. "Thanks."

"You're welcome."

"Be quiet."

"I'm sorry. Your command could not be interpreted as spoken. Please — " "OH, FOR GOODNESS' SAKES! P-29-46."

"Shutting down — *now*."

"Praised be the One Above. Peace and quiet," Ben says, closing his eyes to enjoy it, then opening them and surveying his office with pleasure.

His dear, dear office with its thick carpet and coffee-maker and two walls of glass, all glass, and the city laid out below him. The big, black leather swivel chair and the L-shaped glass desk and the latest and greatest technology and the wires snaking to various outlets around the room.

Ben sighs in contentment. He loves his office.

He shrugs his jacket off and dumps it on a folding chair in the corner. He kicks his shoes off and plops into his chair, shoving himself away from his desk so he zooms across the room to a wall that is bare except for a screen and a pad of colorful buttons. He presses the orange message button, then pushes off again in the direction he came, sliding neatly back into his desk.

He places his feet on the desktop and leans back, wiggling his toes and noticing a hole.

Why in heaven's name do socks get holes? he wonders. What are they doing when he's not paying attention? Wrestling?

And why are there so many messages on his machine every day? These messages running in the background are dull and boring. They lull him into a state of semi-consciousness as the voices drone on…and on…and on.

"Ben, honey, I went to pick up your shirts at the dry-cleaner and the lady there told me that that wine stain wouldn't come out…"

"Hi, Ben, this is Monty from clerking, and I'm checking in on the data research project on pelicans and eating disorders…"

"Hello, this is Sherman. Uh, I was wondering if we could, uh, if at all possible, uh, if you could, uh, give me a, uh, call sometime. I need to discuss…"

"Ben, get on up here right now. I don't know why you're not answering the phone; it's 9:30!" BEEEEEEEEEEEEEEEP.

"End of messages. To repeat, please press…"

Oh, drat, the luck. Typical Gordon. The one day, the ONE DAY he's late, and Gordon calls in.

Ben presses a red button on his keyboard, and he and his chair shoot through a hole that opens up in the ceiling and lands him in his upper office. His upper office with its hardwood flooring and the water cooler that doesn't work and four walls staring blankly back at him. Ben hates this office.

He rises quickly from his leather chair and exits the room into the center chamber of floor 60.

Gordon's office is just to the right of the copy machine. A copper plaque hanging on the door reads: M. Gordon, Chief of Affairs. Ben raps politely on the door.

"Enter!" booms a voice.

Ben turns the knob and steps into Gordon's office, closing the door behind him.

Gordon looks up from the stack of papers he is going through.

"Ben. How delightful!" he says, with a face that shows it is anything but delightful.

"Gordon," says Ben with a nod, sitting down at the chair across from Gordon.

"Yes, what is it, Ben? I haven't got all day, you know."

"You called me up here, Gordon. Quit playing games."

"Hmph. We are prickly today. But, yes, Ben, I did call you up here today. That is correct. I called you up, yes, yes... But why did I do so? Can you answer that?"

"Um, to talk to me."

"But about what?"

"And I'm supposed to know that because...?"

"Because...right. Ben, focus! You were four minutes late today. FOUR MINUTES LATE."

"Correct. Is that why you called me up here?"

Gordon doesn't seem to hear, or perhaps he chooses to pretend not to hear.

"Four minutes late, Ben. Do you know what that means?"

"Is this a trick question?"

"Ben..."

"It means I'm four minutes late."

"Exactly," Gordon says, pouncing on this statement. "You're FOUR MINUTES LATE."

He looks at Ben meaningfully. Ben looks back.

"Four minutes, Ben."

Again Gordon looks at him, his eyebrows raised in pious earnestness.

"I am very sorry," Ben says obligingly.

"So you think, Ben, you think, *I am just four minutes late. What's the big deal?* But four minutes late to work means four minutes late starting work, which means four minutes late to lunch, four minutes late coming home, four minutes late going to bed. Then," and here Gordon pauses for dramatic effect, "then you wake up four minutes late the next day. Your whole life you spend trying to make up those four minutes! And that is a very bad thing! Okay?"

Ben nods patiently. He hesitates to tell Gordon that not everyone in this world runs on a minute-by-minute schedule. He settles on a more appropriate response.

"You know, I could always take off four minutes from lunch." *Or work*, he thinks.

A smirk tugs at the corners of Gordon's mouth, but Ben doesn't care. Let him think he's won.

"You do that," says Gordon.

"All right," Ben says and presses his palms to the sides of his chair, pushing to rise. "See you around, Gordon."

"Not so fast," Gordon says.

With a sigh, Ben settles back down.

"Rob wants you in his office."

"Okay," Ben says, and he attempts to leave once more.

"We're having difficulties with him, Ben. We need your help."

Ben raises an eyebrow. "Difficulties?" he says, and he slumps into his seat.

Gordon nods, cupping his chin in the palm of his hand. He looks up at Ben with the eyes of a stray puppy. Ben is his last hope.

"As you know, we've been expanding a lot these past few years, and that's a good thing."

"Okay…"

"Well, um, see, there's this building. Prime location, beautiful, big…"

"And you want to make it the center, but Rob says he's not moving."

"No, that's not it."

"Oh."

"I mean, it would be nice if we could ALL move out of this dump, but that's not the problem. The problem is, I checked our finances and we have practically no ready money."

"What? What do you mean, 'no ready money'?"

"I don't know. It's being channeled someplace, and Rob won't tell me where."

"So you want me to ask him."

"No. I...you... That's not going to work. You know that; let's not even go there. What I'm just concentrating on at the moment is getting some ready money."

"And...?"

"If we could just market those 'v-lators'!" howls Gordon, smacking his face onto his desk in frustration.

"Oh, come on," Ben says. "Gordon! Not that old argument. You know he won't change his mind."

"Why? Why, Ben, why? Do you know how much we could make? We're sitting on a virtual gold mine!"

"And that gold mine belongs to Rob."

"But Ben, come on. Please. We need to expand. We need cash, and we need it now. If we wait until one of the upcoming projects are finished, I'm going to lose the deal. For a skyscraper off DUDLEY Square! Do you understand what — "

"Gordon," Ben says.

Gordon looks up, his eyes round in desperation. He rakes at the top of his hair, making it stick up in odd angles like a turkey.

"He won't do it," Ben says.

"But you could convince him."

"That's not my job." Ben gets up and opens the office door.

"Sit down, Ben. Siddown now! THIS IS SERIOUS!"

He growls like a wounded animal as Ben calmly shuts the door behind him.

■ ■ ■

The 61st floor officially doesn't exist. A private elevator lifts Ben up from the 60th floor office.

The 61st floor is not so much a floor as a little attic look-out. It is anything but quaint, however, as it is the office of the man in charge of United Morgan Enterprises. Look around and feast your eyes on this lair.

A pyramid of elephant-proof glass and a crystal desk with floating screens everywhere. And at the desk sits Rob, the seventeenth richest man in North America.

When the sun hits the pyramid of glass at the right angle, such as it does now, it refracts the light into a rainbow that bathes the room in magical Technicolor.

Ben steps from the elevator and it disappears into the floor. The carpeting rolls back so you wouldn't ever know there had been an opening there. He walks towards Rob, who is presumably preoccupied with his work on the computer. From his vantage point behind Rob, he can see the joystick and the flashing and the machine gun and Rob's game character ducking behind a wooden crate in a warehouse.

"Bad guy to your left," says Ben.

Rob's character lifts his gun, and in seconds the bad guy is lying on the floor, riddled with holes, blood spurting in every direction.

"Love the graphics," Ben says dryly.

"It's a newer version of the old one. They fiddled with a couple things."

"You mean they changed it from grosser to grossest."

"It's amazing, and it's not even on the market yet," Rob says with a smirk.

"Hmmm," says Ben. "You missed the secret room."

"Where?"

"Inside the stack of crates back there — see?" Ben points his finger at a spot on the computer screen. "You can smash through that brown one. NO! The one to your left. Left, LEFT; that's your right!"

"Oops. Hey, how did you know about this place?"

"Mike showed me."

"Yeah, but how did Mike know about it? Why would he go smashing through crates like that?"

"This is my son we're talking about."

"Destructo-maniac genius?"

"You got it."

"OH, LOOK — a freaky thing with no head!"

Ben rolls his eyes. "Rob, can you bear to pause the game for a couple minutes?"

"Sure," says Rob, smiling in a charitable manner. He pauses the game. "What can I do for you?"

"I'm sorry?"

"What?"

"Rob, I already went through this game with Gordon."

"Went through what?"

"Omigosh. Nothing." Ben sighs. "You called me up, Rob."

"Did I? Oh, yeah, that's right, I did. Call you up. How come…? How come I called you up?"

Ben slumps down onto a chair next to Rob and rubs the flesh between his eyebrows. Another fine day at the office.

CHAPTER 2
KEHILLATH RABBI NORTON

Surrounding the edges of MBU campus are numerous identical houses. Street after street of brown and red houses that over the years have expanded to something that is fondly called by students, "Shantytown." There is also a laundromat, a grocer, and a Loblaws. And there, look there, at the very end of Cherry Street, are two houses, both owned by the same man.

Two houses? Well, maybe he rents one out to some university workers. Some people do it in this town. It's not THAT odd.

But wait. What's that on the lawn of one of the houses? It's some sort of billboard... It reads: "Yom Kippur services FREE, inquire inside" and below that: "Minchah 6:15 Sunday-Thursday."

Minchah...? Oh, I've heard of Minchah. It's, um,

actually, it's this, uh, rare, exotic dish from the Bahamas. Ya! And, um, sailors of the, uh, the, uuuuuuuuuuuhhhh, British... Paratroopers ate it to prevent scurvy. What do you mean? No, it is expensive; you're right. But the queen kind of got it at a discount because, because, er, it's a long story. No, not now; I'll have to tell you some other time, sorry, because otherwise you might miss him! Look, the man in the weird hat — see?

Across the street at the second house, the screen door slams closed behind Rabbi Norton.

"Bye, Abba!" a five-year-old screams from a window above the garage.

Rabbi Norton waves cheerfully. He crosses the street and walks briskly across the other lawn, pausing briefly to eye the sign, then hurrying on. Already he can see Dan and Lem chatting by the front door.

"Morning, *Rabosai*," he says, fishing deep down in his pants pockets for the keys. He pulls them out and they jangle merrily in his grasp. He finds the silver one and unlocks the door, holding it open for the other men, who continue chatting. Lem is looking straight ahead as he gestures, brows puckered. Dan is slightly pink with restrained laughter.

"Coming in?" asks Rabbi Norton.

Dan looks up. "Hey!" he says. "Good morning, Rabbi! Lem's telling me about his furnace."

"Oh?" says Rabbi Norton, placing his hand on Dan's shoulder and steering him inside. "*Nu*, what about Lem's furnace?"

Dan opens his mouth to respond, but what comes out is a bark of laughter. He clamps his hand hurriedly over his mouth, snickering behind it. Rabbi Norton turns to Lem.

"What about the furnace?" he says.

Lem shrugs. "It exploded."

"Exploded," Rabbi Norton says. Behind him, Dan cackles.

"Again," says Lem with a sigh.

"Again?" Rabbi Norton blanches.

Dan howls, clutching his belly hysterically. "He," he gasps out, "he put, hahahahaha, Lem thought, hahaha, he thought that he'd save some money, so he…" and that's as far as he gets. He grips the doorpost for support and shades his eyes with one hand, looking down at the floor. His shoulders shake up and down, but he laughs so hard, there is no sound.

Rabbi Norton tugs at the ends of his beard in perplexity.

"*Oy vey iz mir*. How did the furnace explode?" he asks.

Lem jams his hands deep into his pockets and scuffs his shoe against the doorpost.

"It just did," he says, then ducks his head and slinks into the shul.

"Was anyone hurt?" Rabbi Norton calls after him, but Lem just shrugs without turning around.

Rabbi Norton gazes silently at Dan, who is busy rubbing his eyes, a grin still dancing on his lips.

"What you find amusing is another's misfortune."

The tone is soft and sincere. Dan uses heroic effort not to roll his eyes.

"I think Lem might have been offended," Rabbi Norton continues.

"Offended that I didn't believe his fairy tale?"

"*Oy*, Danny…"

Dan throws his hands up in defeat. "Rabbi Norton," he says in a high-pitched, melodramatic tone, "you are so right. I'm sorry. I'll go apologize right away."

"Great idea," Rabbi Norton enthuses.

Dan tries not to laugh. Either Rabbi Norton is completely naïve, or he has a good covering of rhinoceros skin. But you couldn't hate the fellow, not even if you wanted to, not even if you tried.

And so Dan enters the shul, conscious of Rabbi Norton's watchful gaze from the doorway. He puts his arm around Lem's shoulder and quietly says, "It was a little funny, that's all, Lem."

Lem shrugs. "I know."

"Yeah, but the rabbi thought you were serious about the explosion."

"I WAS serious. It did explode. Basically. Maybe. Sort of…"

Dan sighs. "You've got to be careful with him, you know? He's completely clueless."

But Dan is wrong. Very wrong.

■ ■ ■

It takes a while, but slowly, slowly the *minyan* forms. Hersh and Judge Davis and Bob and Chaim and Zev with five of his sons. Still they wait.

Professor Koor shows up at the last possible second, screeching to a halt, the front wheel of his Smart car rolling over the curb.

He mutters something about getting ready for the new semester and fire hydrants coming out of nowhere as he takes a seat near the window.

Rabbi Norton beams at him, then walks to the front of the room. He opens his siddur to the correct place, then slaps twice on the *bimah*. Silence falls instantaneously.

He turns to face the room. "A few announcements before we begin. Firstly, this Shabbos I'd like to invite everyone to a *shalosh seudos* here."

Smiles all around.

"It will start at 5:45, SHARP."

This elicits a few good-humored chuckles.

"I'm serious this time," says Rabbi Norton, a smile pulling at his cheeks. "Oh, and Minchah from now on will be at 5:15. Is this a problem for anyone?"

Bob clears his throat. "I'll probably do Minchah in the city then, starting now."

Chaim raises a finger.

Rabbi Norton nods his head. "*Nu*, we'll be two down, but if we can rely on Zev's — "

"We'll be there," says Zev, spreading his arms to squeeze the shoulders of the two closest sons, who grin. "You can count on us."

"*Baruch* Hashem!" And without further ado, Rabbi Norton starts the *davening*.

■ ■ ■

Davening ends, and Hersh rushes off to his city job. Zev loads up his brood into the car to head back to Kitchener, the neighboring town.

Judge Davis and Professor Koor leave together, discussing Hybrid cars, corn, and ethanol gas.

Chaim is pacing the hall outside the shul-room, yammering a mile a minute on his cell phone, gesturing broadly with one hand and stuffing a doughnut in his mouth with the other.

Lem wraps his *tefillin* and kisses them before placing them slowly back in their bag.

Bob and Dan are in the kitchen discussing the benefits of humor in advertising versus sophistication. Heated arguments are punctuated by slurps of instant coffee.

"It depends on the product you're trying to market. You're not —" SLURP — "you're not going to sell fountain pens by being funny."

"But everyone –" SHLSHLSH — "likes a laugh when — "

"Not necessarily!"

"Let me finish a sentence and you'd understand what I'm trying to — AHHHH! OUCH, HOT, HOT, HOT!" Splashing and scuffling and the ripping of paper towels.

Rabbi Norton opens the broom closet near the storage room and stoops down, picking up a metal box. He opens it and selects his numbers. He exits the shul and walks to the sign on the lawn.

He removes "6:15" and pulls out "5:15." He pauses to take a deep breath, getting a lungful of smoke from a passing car. Five-fifteen Minchah means fall is coming, but the weather is still nice.

He looks around, seeing nothing to warn of the new season. The trees are still covered in green; birds still caw at each other across telephone wires. Next door he sees Professor Graham's mother tottering down the front path with her walker. He waves vigorously.

"Taking a walk?" he calls out.

"Getchour ugly hand away from me," she snaps, scuffling down the road in the opposite direction.

Rabbi Norton shrugs. "It's beautiful weather for a walk!" he calls after her and snaps "5:15" into place. Pity about the days getting shorter. He always did love summer...

"I watered down the oil," says a voice behind him.

He jumps, then hurriedly straightens his hat and turns. Lem stands there, winding a *tzitzis* string tightly around his finger.

"It didn't really explode, exactly. Just kind of simmered and steamed and stuff. Like chicken soup."

"I, um...Well, *baruch* Hashem that was all! I was scared for you."

"Naaaw, no explosions, Rabbi. But it does sound better saying exploded, don't you think?"

Rabbi Norton keeps a neutral expression. Maybe now is not the time to talk about *emes*. *Yoish*, maybe later... Should he call lunchtime? No, lunchtime he needed to go to Kinko's and photocopy some Shema cards...

"Well, I'll be seeing you. Thanks for your concern and all."

Rabbi Norton blinks, then smiles and waves goodbye.

"Oh," says Lem, "I almost forgot to ask. My son's coming for Labor Day weekend. Is it okay if I bring him for *davening*?"

"*Oish*, what sort of question is that? It would be more than okay, Lem. How old is he?"

"Twelve."

"*Nu*? What's happening with a Bar Mitzvah?"

"Ya, that's kind of why I want him to come, y'know. It's not until the spring, though. Anyway, goodbye."

"Goodbye, Lem. *Kol tuv*," says Rabbi Norton, waving at Lem's receding back before realizing that he forgot to ask if the mother is Jewish... Ah, well, next time.

He re-enters the shul, almost colliding with Dan and Bob who are leaving together for work. He steps outside to let them pass. Then he enters, stooping down once more. He returns the numbers to their correct places in the metal box. The smell of coffee teases him, and he goes and fixes himself a cup. He settles himself comfortably in a kitchen chair and stares dreamily out the window, clutching the coffee cup in both hands. Life in Shantytown is tough, but he wouldn't give it up for all the money in the world.

CHAPTER 3
DINNER TIME

Such is the fate of a fish foolish enough to swim into fishing waters: It is caught; it is gutted; it is rinsed, chopped, doused in wine, and sprinkled with spices; it is bounced on a frying pan with onions and red peppers; it is slapped onto a plate and ground finely between the teeth of ravenous humans and mercilessly swallowed in a single gulp.

Rob swallows his mouthful of fish in a single gulp.

"Delicious, Claire," he says, smacking his lips. "Open a restaurant."

"Oh, shush," says Claire, snapping a dishtowel at him. She busies herself searching the contents of the fridge, turning her face to hide her pleased smile. She loves it when Rob comes to dinner.

Behind her back, Rob sighs in contentment. Ben

looks over at him and frowns. That little flatterer. He is not to be outdone.

"As good as ever, my dear," he says.

"Yes, with the taste of heaven," says Rob.

"And the scent of, of, onions," Ben counters.

From deep within a bunched-up hoodie comes a snort.

"Keep your comments to yourself, you junior delinquent," Ben threatens, piercing a piece of fish with the handle of his fork, then looking down at it in surprise.

"I apologize, ancient one," says a voice as flat and lifeless as cardboard.

"I'm forty-eight!" Ben wipes the back of his fork with a napkin.

"Yes."

"That is not OLD!"

"If you say so."

"Ghaaa!!!!! I demand to know whose kid this is!" says Ben, stuffing a forkful of fish in his mouth and chomping it mightily.

Rob has been quietly scraping the last vestiges of food from his plate, oblivious to everything else. He hums a song of no apparent tune to himself, enjoying Claire's cooking. Now he looks up and notices Ben pointing a piece of celery threateningly at the lump of fabric and bony limbs sitting across from him. Which reminds him —

"MIKE!" he booms, heaping another portion of vegetables onto his plate. "Ben tells me you know some good cheats for BladeCraft IV."

"Hmmm."

"C'mon, how about showing your good old Uncle Rob some tricks of the trade, eh?"

For the first time that meal, Mike looks up. He gazes right through Rob in blatant disinterest. Then he turns his attention back to the piece of pepper he has been chasing around his plate with the tip of his knife.

The side door opens, then slams. A pattering of energetic footsteps and Chad appears.

"Hey, Uncle Rob!" he says, walking over to him and shaking his hand firmly.

Claire hands him a plate, and he pecks her on the cheek.

Chad sits down at his place next to his brother and nudges him with an elbow. "Did you know Uncle Rob was coming for dinner?" he whispers. The lump chooses not to respond. Chad shrugs, then beams a 600-watt smile at everyone. He attacks his food with vigor.

"Yum. Sorry I'm late; busy day at work today," he says. He chews for a couple seconds before asking, "What'd I miss?"

"Mike's going to get me to the next level of BladeCraft," Rob says, beaming.

"Oh, ya? Is, uh, Mike aware of this?"

This gets a hint of a smile from Mike.

"Of course — me and Mike are best buddies. He'd love to help me. Right, Mike?"

Mike is silent.

"Right?"

Silence.

"Right?"

Chad feels Mike squirm next to him, and he knows Rob will get his way. This time.

"Right, Mike?"

Mike grits his teeth.

"Mike, you alive?"

"Fine," he mutters.

"Oho, boy! This is gonna be great!" And Rob rubs his hands together in delight. He actually rubs his hands together.

Mike recedes further into his sweatshirt. "Mother," he says, "kindly restrain your brother."

Claire hides her amusement. "Rob's just letting off the stress of all that hard work he's doing nowadays."

"Ha! Hard work!" says Ben.

Claire withers him with one look.

"I think this is a wonderful idea," she says.

"I can't wait," says Rob. "Me and Mike, just chillin' together. Having a good time...." He reaches out an arm and places it around Mike's shoulder, giving it a squeeze, then letting his arm and hand rest there as he uses his other hand to shovel more vegetables into his mouth. He starts up his tuneless song once more.

"If you don't take your hand off my shoulders in two point four seconds," says Mike, "I will bite it."

Rob snatches his arm away as if he'd been scalded.

Ben chortles into his milk.

■ ■ ■

"Please pass the salt. Please pass the salt. Pass the salt, pass the salt, pass the salt, pass the salt, pass the salt, pass the — "

Rabbi Norton plunks the saltshaker down in front of Tzvi.

"Thank you," says Tzvi and then proceeds to shake half the contents of the saltshaker over his chicken.

"Tzvi," says Mrs. Norton, "you don't trust me to make sure the meat is kosher?"

"S'yummy like this," is Tzvi's response. He clutches the bone sticking out of the *polka* with his fist and opens his mouth. His teeth protrude outwards like a lion ready to chomp down on its prey.

Rabbi Norton hands Tzvi a knife.

Tzvi snaps his mouth closed. He examines the knife as one might examine an alien from Planet Zurg who shows up at the Shabbos table.

"This is a knife," explains Rabbi Norton.

Tzvi shrugs and stabs at his chicken.

BANG, CLASH, KSHHH, KSHHHH!

"Yanky, no," says Mrs. Norton, jumping up from her seat. Yanky sits on the floor in shock as Mrs. Norton tosses pots and spoons back into their rightful places.

"Eeh," he says, scrunching up his face to let out a howl.

"Oh, come," says Mrs. Norton. "Would you like some chicken wicken?"

Yanky looks up at his mother curiously.

"Yeah? Some yummy chicken?" Mrs. Norton scoops him up and seats him in his highchair, snapping the tray into place in front of him.

She takes a small *polka* from the serving tray and begins pulling it into miniscule shreds for Yanky.

"Minna," says Rabbi Norton.

"Mmm-hmm?"

"Did you get a call from my mother today?"

"No, not today."

"Okay. Thank you."

"You're welcome. Oh, but you know who did call?"

"Who?"

"That girl from Lakespur, the one I met when — "

"Moh, moh."

"— More chicken for Yanky? What a big boy! — the girl I met when I was mailing a package for Etty."

"And what did she say?"

"Well, turns out she's free Thursday, and — Tzvi, not so close to the edge; it's going to fall — she wants to come over. I told her I'd explain some things. She wanted to know about *shtreimlach*, I think it was."

"Wonderful, wonderful," says Rabbi Norton. "Would she be

interested in a Shabbos, do you think?"

"Who knows? But she's such a nice girl. So friendly. If not for the jeans, you would think she was from Bais Yaakov..."

"*Boirei nifashois rabbois v'chesroinan al kol mah shebarasah l'hachayos bahem nefesh kol chai, boruch Chey Ha'oilamim,*" Tzvi says in an enthusiastic voice. Rabbi Norton rubs his ear.

"Amen," says Mrs. Norton. "Now put your plate in the dishwasher and get ready for bed."

"I don't WANT to go to — "

"Not yet, not yet. You can play a little after you put your pajamas on, okay?"

Tzvi nods and hops off his chair. He turns to leave the room.

"Uh-uh. PLATE," Mrs. Norton reminds him, and Tzvi returns to the table to get his plate.

With Tzvi gone, the room seems somehow slower, sleepier, and quieter. It would almost be peaceful were it not for Yanky, who was using the back of his father's neck as target practice.

Rabbi Norton scoots his chair away from the line of fire. Then he closes his eyes, his hands resting on his stomach in contentment.

"So, Moish, did you go past the campus recently?" asks Mrs. Norton, untying Yanky's bib.

"Well, uh, let's see... The last time I went by it was Monday morning. Does that count as recently?"

"Not for this it doesn't. Maybe you can go tomorrow, yeah, Moish? No, Yanky, don't touch." She sits Yanky on the counter next to the sink and wipes his face with a dishcloth.

"What's there?"

"Hmmm?"

"What's on campus that I should go see?"

"OH. Oh. One second." She settles Yanky on the floor with a pretzel to gnaw on.

"What's there?" Rabbi Norton repeats.

"Students."

"What? Already? I thought it was Sunday they're coming. It IS Sunday they're coming."

"Yes, but there's a new rule. The students from out of the country have to come five days earlier. If there's a problem with their passports or documents, at least they won't miss the first day of school for it anymore, because they find out about it sooner."

Rabbi Norton nods. "It's a good idea," he says.

"They do something smart every once in awhile, surprisingly. So tell me, are you going to go over tomorrow?"

"For sure," says Rabbi Norton. "I'll print out some signs tonight, if you're not using the computer."

"No, no, you go right ahead. Maybe we'll get a guest for Shabbos."

"Maybe, maybe. And invite the girl you were telling me about."

"Shelly? Well, Hashem split the Yam Suf. These things happen sometimes, you know. She might very well agree. And it's the perfect week for guests."

"Why this week, specifically?"

"Why this week, he asks," Minna says to the walls. She turns to her husband with an amused expression on her face.

"What?" he says, looking from side to side in innocent bewilderment.

"Well, let's see. We just might have enough food this week, seeing as we have the *shalosh seudos* — "

"Oh, right. Right."

"*Gevalt* — you didn't forget to tell the *minyan*, did you?"

"No, no, it just slipped my mind this second..."

"And also Zev's family's going to be here. And this week is the last week his older boys are going to be home, so for sure Frumma is going to cook even more."

Rabbi Norton chuckles. "Fattening them up before yeshiva season. *Oy*, what a woman."

"Moish!" says Minna. "A little bit *avak lashon hara*, yeah?"

Rabbi Norton cringes.

"Sorry, that was a bit harsh... Anyway, regardless, there'll be so much food we'll be drowning in it. And you know as well as I do that young men are ruled by their stomachs, so — "

"Being ruled — that's it!" Rabbi Norton stands up and begins pacing the room, tugging at the ends of his beard.

"Eureka," says his patient *eishes chayil*. "And what are we talking about?"

Rabbi Norton pauses with one foot off the ground. "Oh," he says, smiling at her through the haze of somewhere far, far away, "my *dvar* Torah." And he resumes his pacing.

Mrs. Norton smiles with the unquestioning patience she has developed for herself over the years of her marriage. She gathers crumbs into a neat pile on the counter and nods. "Well, go ahead and use the computer. Like I said, I don't need it tonight."

Rabbi Norton returns to the table and removes his plate. He jams it haphazardly into the dishwasher, his mind clearly somewhere else.

His wife waits until he leaves the room to remove and scrape it.

A slight breeze comes in through the small kitchen window, ruffling the polka-dotted curtains. From the living room she hears her husband singing *chazanus* as the computer chimes its boot-up tune. Tzvi is racing cars on the hardwood floor above her head. The tick-tock, tick-tock of the hall clock makes her feel calm. The streets are empty; the world is still. The outdoor sky is blue, the color blue that only a blue sky can be. It's about seven now…and there is the sun, a low orange globe in the sky. Fall is coming, but it feels like summer. It smells like summer and summer grass.

She sits down in a nearby chair and sighs with pleasure. There are dishes to do, but there is life to live. She could sit forever, watching the sky darken.

In the corner, Yanky pulls a chair down on top of himself and lets out a wail.

CHAPTER 4
WHAT A WONDERFUL DAY

The alarm clock goes off at seven a.m., a malicious, piercing sound that slams into the brain and presses the eyeballs.

In the bed nearby, Claire sits up and squeezes her eyes open and shut a couple times. Then she hops out of bed and into her bunny-rabbit slippers.

From the washroom she can hear a roar of water and squeaking and Ben warbling, "FEEGAROH, DA DA DAUM DEE, DAH OH FEEFEEFEEGA-ROOOOOOOOOOH...."

Claire rubs her temples.

Ben turns off the shower and there is silence, followed shortly by the high-pitched, whirring buzz of a shaver.

Claire stumbles blearily to her closet. She hates her closet. She ought to love it, really she ought to, but it's so big and it's so full of choices, none of which she likes. This outfit makes her look fat; this one makes her ears look green. Maybe a suit. The brown? Yes, the brown one would be perfect, the one with the cute stitching around the pockets. Perfect if she could just find the thing. Where is it? Wasn't it just here yesterday? Yes, it definitely was...not. That's right, it's at the cleaners. The one outfit she wants to wear, and she took it to the cleaners. Of course, that would only be natural, and now what is she supposed to wear?

In the washroom, Ben inspects his nasal hair. With a sigh, he turns to the full-length mirror. He stands with his shoulders back, sucking in his stomach and tightening his bathrobe's belt to cinch at the waist. He admires his smooth-shaven face, the poise and cool-headedness of his stance. He smoothes his hair back with the side of his thumb and thinks to himself that he cuts quite a dashing figure. Hmmm, maybe he should grow a mustache. A nice handlebar one like all those Italian chefs seem to wear... Ha ha, right, like he could ever pull that off.

He turns to leave and slips on the moist floor, clanking his head against a cabinet with a muffled thump and a not-so-muffled scream of pain.

Claire rushes from her closet, blue shoes unbuckled and flapping up and down as she runs. She pounds on the bathroom door.

"Ben?" she yells. "Are you alright?"

"Oh, yes. I'm fine, dear. I just... Never mind. Don't worry."

"What happened?"

"I banged my head against the cabinet."

"Oh...," she says, then blinks. "Wait a second. The cabinets? Why would your head be anywhere near the cabinets? What are you doing down there, Ben? If you're trying to do the plumbing yourself again, heaven help me, but I'm going to bash this door down; do you hear me?"

"No, I'm not doing the plumbing, Claire. Please, just don't worry about me."

"If you say so." Still slightly puzzled, Claire returns to her closet to finish styling her hair.

Ben groans and sits up squeamishly, rubbing the side of his head with the heel of his hand.

He leaves the bathroom and heads directly to his closet. His gray suit, his yellow shirt, his maroon tie, and Ferrogamo dress shoes. He winks at his reflection and then leaves the room. He strides purposely down the spiral staircase, lifting his feet higher than necessary with each step, like a show horse or a wind-up soldier.

Before checking the kitchen for breakfast, he stoops by the front door and peeps through the mail-slot. The porch is empty. Ben frowns.

"Dear!" he calls.

"Yes?" Claire calls back shrilly, through a curtain of hair.

"Did my newspaper come yet?"

"I don't know. Check the front porch."

"I did."

"Then...what am I supposed to tell you?"

"Nothing; never mind. I was just hoping...oh, bother," he puffs his breath out in annoyance and decides Fiber One is not a good idea for breakfast this morning.

He'll have a doughnut and a coffee with cream. The diet can start tomorrow.

In the kitchen he starts the espresso machine and sorts through a box of doughnuts, settling for a whipped cream twist with cinnamon glaze.

Upstairs, Claire has finished parting her hair. In one swift movement, she clamps it to the back of her head securely.

What time is it? Seven-thirty already? In clipped movements, she strolls purposely down the hall and raps on Chad's door.

"Come in," says a voice, loud, clear, and radiating cheerfulness.

She opens the door a crack and peeks in.

"Chad, honey?" she says.

"Oh, good morning, Mother. What can I do for you today?"

"Just checking to make sure you were up. I see you're doing some university prep...?"

"Oh, just a little research for work. But don't worry; I'll be ready to leave on schedule."

"I know you will."

"It's so nice to set things moving early. Morning is the best time for doing work, seeing as-"

"Yes, of course. You carry on. I've got to wake up your younger brother. Wish me luck."

"Glad it's not me," says Chad, then turns back to his binder, tapping a pen against its cover.

"Well, good morning," Claire says, then closes the door.

Chad sighs in relief and dumps the binder off the desk.

Across the hall, Claire hesitates, then opens Mike's door. No need to knock — he wouldn't hear it anyway.

"Mike," she says, though she knows it is futile. She steps further inside, breathing shallowly through her hand. Hesitantly, she plunges through a pile of old socks and notebooks, stubbing her toe. Wincing, she stubbornly advances towards the center of the room. Mike is there somewhere, surely, on the bed... That is the bed, right?

Oh, gross. Claire muffles a squeal of disgust as the heel of her shoe squelches into something sticky. Gritting her teeth, she yanks her foot out. She notices a hockey stick and reaches for it, lifting it by the blade.

"Mike?" she says again, prodding a mass of blanket and dirty socks with the end of the stick.

Beneath the pile, something stirs.

"Time to wake up."

"Mmm."

"Mike, get up this instant!" she shrieks. Knowing now the location of her son, she pokes all the more vigorously in that particular spot.

A rousing snort emerges from the depths, a smacking of lips, a groan. Then silence.

"Chad!" Claire has had enough.

Chad appears in the doorway. He sticks his head in, sniffs, then whips his head back, wrinkling his nose.

"Yes, Mother?" he says.

"Do something. I don't care what. Just get him up." With this, she stalks from the room.

Chad watches her receding back, then turns towards the mountain of chaos. A demonic grin splits his face.

■ ■ ■

The radio carries no news, the television only advertises, and the newspaper... Ben lets the mail-slot fall closed with a resounding bang.

Claire is puttering around in the kitchen. As Ben stands, she walks in. A mug is clutched between two manicured hands.

"What's the matter?" she asks, eyeing her husband's clenched fists wearily.

"That paperboy — " is all Ben can get out; then, "Is that the coffee from the espresso machine?"

"Mmm-hmm," says Claire. "Thanks. It was very thoughtful of you."

A frown creases Ben's brow. "You're welcome," he says.

He returns to the kitchen to restart the coffee. From upstairs he hears a crash, a smash, and the scuffling of feet. The light fixture above his head sways lazily. Vaguely concerned, he makes his way to the bottom of the stairwell, narrowly missing contact with Chad, who streaks past him at a speed illegal in all states but Texas.

Mike is close behind in pajama shorts and tee, face beet-red.

Looking closely, you might imagine smoke rising from his forehead. But that is ridiculous, as well as impossible. Of course it isn't smoke. It's steam.

Chad has run into the washroom off the living room. The door is locked. Mike pounds his fists against it.

"Open the door, Chad," he states in a threateningly calm monotone. "Open the door. I'll pound your brains out."

"Oh, that's going to make me open it."

Claire walks into the living room. "What's going on?" she says.

Mike lets out a strangled grunt and slinks out of the room, leaving a trail of water droplets behind him.

"Mike," says Claire, "get dressed."

But Mike is going back to bed, and nothing will stop him. Not anything, not anyway, no how, no —

"Or I can always get you the same clothes that Chad buys."

Mike goes upstairs to get dressed.

Slowly, the door of the bathroom opens, and Chad peeps his head cautiously around the doorpost.

"All clear," he hears Ben call from the foyer. Chad walks out of the living room and sees him stooped by the mail-slot.

"Dad," he says. Ben gets up. He does not look happy. Perhaps Chad should have waited for a better moment for this, but it's too late to back down now.

"I need a new laptop," he says.

Ben shrugs. "So get one," he says. "What's the problem?"

"Um…"

"Did you lose the card I gave you?"

"No. But there's this incredible model that I know your company is working on. And that's the one I want, you understand?"

Ben narrows his eyes. "And you know about this because…"

"Oh. Well, Rob gave Mike one and — "

"WHAAAT?!" Ben's mind races. He cannot believe it. What was Rob thinking?! The computer wasn't due to be released until three to four months from now. No one was supposed to receive a copy. Even he hadn't taken one.

That man has no interest in his company, in its well-being or in its profit.

"So, can you get it for me, Dad?" says Chad.

But Ben can't hear him over the roaring in his ears. That computer is his, HIS creation. Okay, not actually his computer, per se. But it was *he* who slaved over it, *he* who made sure deadlines were met and people were doing the best jobs they could do. And there goes Rob! Okay, granted it's his company, but it's not like he has any interest in it. It's not as if Rob even CARES about what's going on. And yet, occasionally, he'll just DO something. Maybe it's Rob's company, and maybe Gordon is second-in-command, all this technically. But everyone knows who *really* runs the show. It's HIM. Ben Horatio Burns. And nobody, NOBODY is allowed to just do whatever they want.

He stomps into the kitchen, almost colliding with Mike. Mike holds a mug in his hand. Ben checks the espresso machine and, yes indeed, yes, it is empty once more.

With a roar of frustration, he spins on his heel and heads to the door, yanking it open. The front porch is empty. WHERE IS THAT PAPERBOY?

"Have a great day," Chad calls after him as he heads down the front walkway. "Don't forget about the computer."

Ben grumbles and shakes his head.

His briefcase! Oh, what does he need it for? He never puts anything in it anyway. He looks over his shoulder at Chad and tells him with his eyes in no uncertain terms that he is not getting that laptop.

He feels disoriented and angry and impatient, and it's not even nine yet.

Fine. Who cares about coffee, who cares about paperboys, who cares about sons who are disrespectful and doctor's orders and gray hairs.

Who cares about anything anymore. But Ben has a company to run. He reaches into his pocket and presses a button on his key tag. The Jaguar blinks its headlights and chirps merrily.

"Oh, be quiet," says Ben.

CHAPTER 5
SPARKS

"Hey, Jew."

Rabbi Norton pauses, fingers frozen in place, pinching the thumbtack. He does not choose to turn from the bulletin board. Rather, he stares straight ahead at its grainy, pocked surface.

"Whatcha doin', man, huh?"

He feels a presence closer still at his back; he smells axe deodorant.

"Blessin' our school, holy guy?"

He hears raucous laughter behind him, and he knows this boy isn't backing down anytime soon. Not with a group of encouraging buddies at his back.

Rabbi Norton pushes his glasses up his nose and tucks the sheaf of papers under his arm. He finishes sticking the thumbtack into his flyer.

Then he turns. Calmly. Patiently. He can understand their curiosity, their wonder at a man dressed in a black hat and suit. A man who looks to be from a different galaxy, far from their world of gray sweat pants and oversized tee-shirts and preppy cable-knit sweaters.

He can understand their curiosity. He was once curious himself.

"Yes?" he says.

The speaker wears a skull tee-shirt, a Mohawk, and a twisted sneer across his pimply face.

"I asked a question; you got a problem answerin'? You deaf or somethin'?"

"Oh, no, not at all. I am pleased to say that my ears are in remarkably good health, and I'd be more than happy to answer any question of yours."

The boy's eyebrows shoot upwards. He tilts his head slightly to the side and regards Rabbi Norton with hardened eyes. Evidently, this is a gaze meant to disconcert, a gaze meant to inform a person that they are scum not worthy of anyone's attention. Rabbi Norton is quite amused.

"What is it you wanted to know? What I was doing...?"

"Whatever, Jew. I don't care about your dumb Jewish things, Jew."

"Yes, I am a Jew, correct."

"Shut it," says the boy, grunting in disgust and stomping off.

But Rabbi Norton is not concerned, because he has noticed something this boy has not. This exchange was calculated; this exchange was planned. Now the boy is gone and his group is gone, but one boy is not.

It is a cheerful-looking boy, the boy you see sometimes in tough gangs and wonder to yourself what he's doing there.

A nice boy, a friendly boy, a happy boy. The type of boy that likes to wear loud Hawaiian shirts and goofy hats. The boy who everyone needs around, and everybody has one such a person in their life, if they have any such life at all.

"Are you Jewish?" asks Rabbi Norton, cutting straight to the point.

The boy's eyes flicker from side to side. He nods slightly, quickly.

"Rabbi Norton." He sticks out his hand in greeting.

"Jeremy," says the boy, automatically flicking a mock salute.

Rabbi Norton lets his arm swing down to his side. "I'd like to get to know a fellow Jew. Doing anything Friday night?"

Jeremy shrugs and rolls his eyes. He turns to leave, but before he is too far, he calls over his shoulder, "Nice hat." Then he is gone.

Rabbi Norton fingers the felt rim of his hat distractedly. *Nice hat...* That wasn't... an Australian accent, was it? He smiles to himself as he removes the sheaf of papers from under his arm and heads off towards the bulletin boards by the pool area.

He smiles to himself because he knows something even Jeremy doesn't.

Jeremy will be back. Jeremy is going to experience a Shabbos.

■ ■ ■

"Right, I know, but...K, so what if you're not ready to do all this stuff, you know what I'm saying? Like, maybe I could do this whole kosher thing, but not, um, like not the long skirt, hello-I'm-an-Amish-freak type of weirdness."

"Wow," says Minna. "Keeping kosher is a HUGE step. Of course it would be ridiculous for anyone to expect you to turn your entire life around in three seconds. Life just doesn't work like that."

"I know, totally! Like, that was what I was thinking to myself, you know? Like, I'm really into this...I really am, but it's totally SCARY. Like, my dad's going to totally flip when he finds out. He's sooooooooo paranoid. When I split up with Greg — get this — he sent me to a psychiatrist! I mean, for goodness' sake, I'm nineteen, and, like, maybe it's time for me to run my own life, hello?" She rolls her eyes, picking at her purple nail polish.

Judging by how much Shelly still talks about Greg, maybe her father wasn't so off in his decision-making. But Minna doesn't say this. Instead, she looks into Shelly's eyes and asks, "Do you miss Greg at all?"

"Yeah," says Shelly, and her mouth twists into a half-smile, and her eyes wander to gaze somewhere off in the distance, somewhere far, far away. "I kind of liked the guy. He was so REAL, but...like, G-d is so much real-er, if you know what I'm saying."

Minna looks at Shelly. Shelly looks out the window.

It must have been hard. It's not so pleasant to break off a relationship like that. It takes willpower and strength of character that is beyond most people. Minna reaches across the table and covers Shelly's delicate hand with hers.

"Did you ever ask him if he was Jewish? Maybe if he was — "

"No. His grandfather was like a Nazi or something. And anyway, it's totally over. He...we...it's done."

"Well," says Minna, and though she knows it probably won't help Shelly much to hear this, she says, "you did the right thing. The right thing is not always the easy thing."

"I'll say. But, so how does this kosher stuff go? Do you think you could teach me?"

"Oh!" says Minna, slapping her forehead. "Right. Come, let me give you some booklets — they really help. And, actually, it's kind of fun in a way, hunting for all those *hechshers*. You'd be surprise how many things are actually kosher — for example, chocolate-covered Rice Krispies. What respectable mother is going to buy that for her children, I ask you..."

■ ■ ■

"Mike, what do you think?" asks Claire, holding up a pair of corduroy slacks.

Mike gazes dispassionately through her.

"Mike, I asked you a question and I would like a response, please."

Chad bounds up behind her. "Mother, how about these?" He holds up a tan suit, a candy-striped tie, and a crisp blue shirt.

Mike chuckles.

"Mike, please," says Claire. "Those are beautiful. And as you can see, CHAD will be ready for university, and you won't. What are you planning on doing? Walking around in pajamas all day?"

Mike shrugs. "Maybe."

"Mike!"

A salesman interrupts with a beaming smile. "Hi! Is there anything I can help you with?"

Mike eyes the false cheerfulness aloofly. He turns his eyes to look out of the store at the people crowding the high-end mall for back-to-school shopping, prancing about like overstuffed peacocks on parade.

"Actually," he can hear Chad say, "I was wondering if you had this in a 36. There's a…"

His mother is still browsing through the racks, searching for something hideous to ply him with. Mike shakes his head in disgust and recedes further into himself.

All talking becomes a buzz; all customers become a blur of colors. And there, across and to the side of this store, is another store that catches his eye.

Flashes of fluorescent lights and a graffiti-style sign and a salesclerk with a shaved scalp. Involuntarily, Mike's feet begin moving towards it. The booming beat and cemented floor so different from the muted new-age music and soft carpeted units where sleazy salesmen attempt to sell you $3,000 suits.

Someone brushes by his elbow.

"Mike!" says a voice.

He looks up. Who…oh, it's Frank.

"Good to see you, man."

He blinks in greeting.

"Listen, Bruce's parents are out of town, did you hear?"

He nods curtly.

"C'mon, buddy, you know what that means. PARTY! You're coming, right?"

Mike regards Frank's beaming face with silent curiosity.

"I'm picking you up tomorrow night, nine o' clock. Be ready."

"For what?"

Frank laughs loudly and pounds Mike heartily on the back. Disappearing through the crowd, he calls over his shoulder, "Tomorrow, nine o' clock — don't forget!" Then he is gone.

Mike rubs his back sullenly.

CHAPTER 6
SPELT CHALLOS

"Back, more, a little more. STOP! Forward..."

Rabbi Norton closes his *sefer* and peeks through the kitchen curtains. A warm smile passes over his face. Zev and his *mishpachah* are here.

Zev's wife is on the shul lawn, waving her arms wildly, directing Zev's parking. Zev narrowly misses the billboard. Rabbi Norton winces.

The side door of the van slides open and a troop of boys pile out, followed by a perky five-year-old girl.

Rabbi Norton can hear the front door slam closed. Minna is running down the porch steps and across the street.

"Frumma!" she calls out.

"Oh, helloooooo, Minna! It's so good to see you."

"Good to see you, too! Did your boys eat lunch?"

"Yes, they ate in the car. But let me tell you, we're never doing that again. Either we don't leave so early from now on, or they starve. Such a mess they made, Minna. I am not happy about this — *Gevalt*, what is he doing?!"

Tzvi is currently being dangled upside down by his ankles by six-foot-tall Shmuli. "MOMMY, LOOK AT ME!" he howls, red-faced.

Minna smiles serenely, "Oh, I see," she says. "You're so high up, *tzadikel*."

"So long as you're okay with it," says Frumma. She lets out a booming laugh and tosses a beefy arm around Minna's neck. "Come, I made a little something for the meal."

Minna allows herself to be led towards the van, where they are met by Rabbi Norton.

"Where's Zev?" he asks.

"Zev? Zev? Probably inside organizing his ties by color, if I know my husband."

Rabbi Norton nods his thanks and enters the shul.

"And how do you like that? No 'hello,' no 'how are you' … Men!"

"He's lost in a Torah thought," says Minna. "He'll be friendlier by the meal."

"He'd better be," says Frumma, "because I baked some of that spelt challah he liked so much last week, and I tell you, did it come out good…!"

■ ■ ■

Spelt Challos

The shul is quiet; the shul is still. But from somewhere upstairs comes a steady, rhythmic BANG, BANG, BANG.

Rabbi Norton scratches behind his ears in perplexity.

"Zev?" he calls.

There is a muffled response. Rabbi Norton's brow creases in concern.

"Zev!"

The banging increases. Rabbi Norton follows the sound up the stairs to the guest apartment.

The bedroom's doorframe shudders with each pound, and Rabbi Norton runs straight to it.

"What's the matter?"

"It's jammed!" says Zev.

"Hold on. I'll get it open." Rabbi Norton jiggles the handle, but it won't turn. He removes his jacket and hat and places them to the side of the door. He rolls up his sleeves, backs up down the length of the hallway, and charges. WHAM! He hits the door head on. This is as effective as an ant jumping on a nail head. Rabbi Norton tries again. Then again.

"Okay," he says finally, swiping his forehead with the back of his hand, "you pull, I push. On the count of three — one, two, THREE!"

Rabbi Norton slams his shoulder against the door repeatedly. On the other side, Zev grasps the doorknob and leans his entire body back, bracing his feet on the carpeted flooring.

There is a crackling, then a snap, and Rabbi Norton stumbles in and trips over Zev, who is stretched out in the middle of the room. They lie in a heap, catching their breaths.

"Whew," says Zev. "I better call in a repairman."

Rabbi Norton chortles and gets to his feet. He reaches his hand towards Zev and helps him up.

"Are you all right, Zev?"

"No."

"Oh, dear, should I — "

"Kidding."

"In that case, do you have a minute to discuss a *chiddush*?" he asks.

Zev brushes the knees of his pants and adjusts his yarmulke. "Yeah, sure, but first let's sneak some samples from the kitchen, ay, Moish?"

"Yes, that sounds like a good idea. But maybe we should ask my wife first before…"

Zev looks at Rabbi Norton. Rabbi Norton looks at Zev.

"No," says Zev, "let's not bother them on a busy Friday. We'll just help ourselves."

"Right," says Rabbi Norton.

■ ■ ■

There are days when Jeremy wishes he wasn't quite so conspicuous. Today is one of them.

Sure, but to be noticed by all and accepted by all is a wonderful thing. However, there are only so many people one can talk to, and there are only so many minutes a day, and maybe, maybe, it's good to be alone sometimes, too.

All Jeremy wants to do is to leave the dorm room unnoticed, and he has to climb out of the window to do so. Because the last thing he needs is Cole to find out what he is about to do...

There he is now, sticking to the sides of buildings as he darts from shadow to shadow. Beads of sweat glisten on his forehead. He checks to make sure the coast is clear before dashing across the gap between the cafeteria and rec hall. Adrenaline courses through his veins. He feels light-headed. He feels scared. Oddly enough, he feels thrilled.

Behold Jeremy Briggs, master of espionage, as he creeps behind dock warehouses in pursuit of a quarry. He cuts a dashing figure in his black cloak and hobnailed boots. A flash of lightning lights up the sky and thunder rocks the very ground, but nary a shiver is emitted by Briggs the fearless. Slowly, slowly, he advances past the creaky boards of a rotting shack...

Oh, man, not good.

Really not good.

Up ahead is a group of boys.

Jeremy looks closer, squinting against the bright sunshine.

Oh, no worries. It's just a bunch of brown-nosing geeks off on a dander to the tech lab. Jeremy detaches himself from the walls and strolls onward, deliberately keeping his eyes zoned somewhere off in the distance. He jams his fists into his pockets and whistles loudly and off-tune. As he passes them by, he salutes and calls out, "Hey, howzit going?"

The others nod companionably back, and he continues on a few paces before melting back into the cool comfort of the shadows.

Trouble is far from over, however, for there is the arts and cuisine house, diagonally across a vast expanse of perfectly pruned grass.

"Come on," he tells himself, "you're nothing but a paranoid little nose blower. You're going to do this sometime anyway. You might as well get it over with. Ready, set…"

And with this, he runs across the wide open space and through the doors into the arts and cuisine house.

There in the lobby is the bulletin board with the sign-up sheet. A few more seconds and it will all be done…

A pen! Oh, apple crumb cake. He figured they'd tie a pen to the sign-up sheet, but evidently not. He pats his cargo pants all over, checking if he by chance stored a pen in a pocket somewhere, but no. It seems as though he's out of luck.

Footsteps fall heavily outside. Someone is coming; where to hide? It's…

ED! The bench…

Hurriedly, he dives for cover, sending up a cloud of dust to envelope him in grime. The footsteps stop nearby, then silence. He flips over onto his back and peers through the wooden slats. Someone clears his throat nearby. Something scratches.

Jeremy watches Ed in surprise as he hesitantly signs his name up for the Kooking Klub. If he has time for cooking, that must mean that he isn't occupied with football… Funny, Ed struck Jeremy as more of the Football Scholarship sort of fellow, but if he isn't, then that must mean he got into MBU on pure brainpower. Never would Jeremy have thought Ed to be smart. Well, of course there has to be something up there in the cranial region to get accepted here in the first place. More than just something, in fact. But without an athletic scholarship, you'd have to be, you've got to be, you...unbelievable. *Never judge a book by its cover*, thinks Jeremy Briggs.

And of all things, the Kooking Klub. Some things are so hard to predict. But it's nice sometimes to know that you have a brother in crime. It's heartening sometimes to know you're not alone, and someone else is doing a two-time between cool and social suicide.

"Ed!" he calls out.

Ed skitters and looks around, eyes racing from side to side, his shoulders hunched.

"Jeremy," he says, "what are you doing under there?"

"Oh. Uh, I dropped my pen and I was looking..." Jeremy eases himself out and stands, brushing at his shorts. "Maybe you have one I can borrow for a sec?"

Ed's eyes narrow. "Ya, I got one," he says.

Jeremy stretches out his hand eagerly. "Put it here, man."

Ed smacks it down into Jeremy's palm with a resounding whack. Seeing Jeremy looking at the Kooking sign-up sheet, he scowls. "I do what I want. I ain't no sissy-boy fruit cake or nothing. I cook. You got a problem with that?"

"No, no problem. I was just about to sign up myself, actually." And Jeremy does so with a flourish. When he is done, he turns around and holds out the pen, winking at Ed.

Ed snatches his pen back, wrenching it from Jeremy's grasp. "You don't gotta go ratting about this to nobody, hear?" he says, eyebrows drawn into a unibrow at the center of his forehead

"Same to you," says Jeremy, massaging his thumb.

Ed grunts and lumbers off.

"See you around sometime," Jeremy calls after him and cackles as Ed slams into the glass door before yanking it open and stumbling off drunkenly.

"What a jerk," says Jeremy to himself. He rubs his nose and reads over the list to see who else has signed up for the club. Something catches the edge of his eye. It is a fluorescent orange flyer with a fringe of numbers at the bottom.

"Are you Jewish?" it reads in size 76 bold letters, font Impact. And below that: "Doing anything Friday night? Come experience a Shabbos! Eat a delicious home-cooked meal and find out more about being Jewish."

"Doing anything Friday, doing, doing..." Where had he heard those words before...? The rabbi, the guy he met when he was with Cole and the gang, the freaky black-hatter. Yeah right, like he's going to; no way is he going to. Uh-uh, goodbye.

Jeremy turns away from the bulletin board. He closes his eyes and turns back. Without knowing why, he stretches out his arm and tears off a number.

■ ■ ■

A car honks outside the house at approximately eight o' clock that evening.

Claire looks up from her book.

"Someone's beeping," she calls.

A door slams upstairs and Chad comes bounding down the steps. He slips across the smooth marble foyer and spins his arms like a windmill to regain his balance. Face flushed, he flings the door open and peers outside.

In the driveway is a flashy blue convertible with the top down. The back seat is crammed with sweaty boys. In the driver's seat is Frank. The seat next to him is open and waiting.

"Hello, gentlemen!" Chad calls out, waving cheerfully.

"Oh, um, hey, Chad," says Frank. "Where's Mike?"

"Oh, he's upstairs."

"Okay..."

"Anything else I can do for you?"

"Are you stupid or something?"

"I'm sorry?"

"Dude, just send him out, alright?"

Chad hesitates in the doorframe for a moment, then disappears into the house.

"Man, I get such a headache even looking at that guy," says Frank rubbing his eyes underneath his sunglasses and slumping deeper into the seat.

Inside the house, Chad hollers up the staircase for Mike.

Mike pokes his head around the banister.

"Some friends for you," says Chad with a shrug.

Mike nods and trudges down the staircase, dipping his head down into his hoodie like a turtle, his face an impassive mask.

He stops at the door. He does not acknowledge the presence of the boys outside.

"Mike!" says Frank, and he flashes his headlights on and off. A huge grin splits his face. "Mike, my man, get on down here!"

The boys in the back seat whoop.

Mike regards the stone steps at his feet with rapt interest.

"Hello? Two words, brother. Par, Tee, remember? Like I told you in the mall? It's gonna be awesome, last one of the summer!"

"No, thanks," says Mike blandly.

"Aaw, c'mon."

In the back seat, faces fall. This scene has been disturbingly habitual lately.

Mike turns around.

"Hey, where you goin'? I'm still talkin'. I'm not finished with you, Burns!"

But Mike is already gone.

"Nuts," says one boy. "We almost had him. He heads off to college and we're just not good enough for him anymore."

Frank hits the steering wheel with the palm of his hand.

"Man," he says. "Well, not much point showing up there without Mike. It'll just be boring."

"Dude, since when is beer boring?" someone pipes up from the back seat.

Someone else chuckles, but it is a joyless chuckle, manic depressive.

"Dang, ah knew ah shoulda brought mah gun," someone mutters in a phony western twang.

"Shut it, all of you," snaps Frank.

Inside the house, Chad watches his brother slump into a couch.

"What did they want?" he asks.

Mike shrugs. "They're going to a party."

"Did you just walk out on them?"

"Walked in."

"You idiot!" says Chad and rushes to the doorway. "Are you folks going to a party?" he calls out.

Frank looks up in horror. "Um, yeah," he says.

"Well, it doesn't look like Mike will be coming, but I'd be glad to join you."

"No," Frank says, sitting bolt upright in his seat and snatching wildly at the stick shift. The convertible screeches backwards out of the crescent driveway, leaving a cloud of dust in its wake as it turns the corner by the next block, still in reverse.

Chad stares after it.

Five minutes later, he still stands on the cold stone steps, gazing blankly at an empty road in the fading light of the day.

CHAPTER 7
SHABBOS

Captain Briggs stands behind the wheel, knuckles loose and easy, hair plastered to his forehead, as he leads his ship straight into an oncoming wave. It breaks high above the mainsail, water rushing down and sweeping away all that is not secured on deck. His men perfectly stowed below deck, himself lashed to his wheel, Captain Briggs sneers in the face of death. Thunder crashes, lightning flashes. A demonic gleam lights up his eyes. He howls his defiance. He is invincible. He will neither hesitate nor pause.

He pauses, one foot raised on the bottom step of the porch. His heart flutters up to the corner of his jaw. It is a strange feeling, to be sure, he thinks. It's a feeling he doesn't quite recognize, a fear, a, a, shyness, yes, that's the word.

He wonders what it will be like. He tells himself it's not too late to turn back yet. He is a bit early, anyway...

It's weird in a way. He never feels uncomfortable crashing at random people's houses, eating their food, chatting with their mothers. Why should it make a difference whether it's a religious freak or not? He has a friend, Tom, who's Catholic... No, the problem isn't the people, but if it isn't, then what's making him feel so strange?

But when was the last time he'd actually been invited? Being invited...does that mean he has to be more formal? Should he have brought flowers? Well, it's way too late now, which is a shame because he feels obligated to make an impression. He wishes he'd never made the phone call.

He's not going to turn back now, though. He's just going to do this thing, and then it will be over.

He takes a deep breath and squares his jaw. In bold steps, he takes the stairs and raps on the screen door. The actual front door is open and he can hear chattering and giggling from somewhere inside. No one comes. Again he knocks, then yanks the screen door open and sticks his head inside.

"Hello? Anyone home?" he yells.

"In the kitchen," someone calls.

He follows the sound of voices.

A group of ladies sit around a table, some with children on their laps, some holding little books.

"Oh, hello," says the woman at the head of the table, "you must be Jeremy."

Jeremy smiles cheekily. "Hiya," he says. "Where's the rabbi?"

A large woman turns in her chair and beams up at him. "He left for shul a while ago. They stay there a bit after *davening*... He should have been home by now. But I expect you might be wanting the company of men. Tzvi will take you."

"Oh. Yes," says the first lady. "Tzvi!" she calls. "Tzvi!"

A little boy in black shorts clatters down the stairs and into the kitchen. A girl in pigtails and a lacy pink dress trails like a shadow behind him.

"What?"

"Let's try that again. Tzvi?"

Tzvi looks down at his shoes, wrinkling his button nose sheepishly. "Yes, Ima?"

"I'd like you to take our guest to Abba, please."

"Okay, come," Tzvi says and latches on to Jeremy's cargo pants.

Jeremy allows himself to be led outside and across the street.

"Is Rabbi Norton your dad?" he asks as they walk through a lawn towards a red-brick house.

"No, he's my Abba."

"I see. I'm Jeremy."

"Are you going to sleep over?"

"Well, no. I'm going back to my dorm. But I'm staying for the whole meal. How's that?"

Tzvi cocks his head to the side and thinks for a moment before nodding his head solemnly. "You're sitting next to me."

"Am I?"

"Yes. We're eating in my house, and there's this family; they are the Cohens. They always eat with us on Shabbos, because they don't have Jews in their place where they live. So I asked my Abba if you could sit with me, not them, and he said you'd probably want to sit with older people, but I said you want to sit next to us, because grown-ups are boring, and Abba said we should let you decide."

"Hmm. Goody, I can't wait," says Jeremy and bonks Tzvi on the head.

Tzvi smoothes his hair down with a scowl that betrays a lopsided grin of pleasure. He opens the door to the shul and leads Jeremy down a hallway to a crowded room of men wearing black jackets and black hats.

"My Abba's by the front," Tzvi whispers noisily. "You can't talk to him now, because he's davening."

"Um, he's, uh, what?"

"SHHHHHHH!!!!"

"Right, right," Jeremy whispers. "What's he doing, again?"

"Oh. Sorry. He's praying. But soon he'll be done, and then we can eat."

"All right, food! Put it here, buddy." Jeremy holds out his palm for a high five.

Tzvi shakes it.

Jeremy blinks.

"Bye-bye, I'll see you soon." And with a wave of his hand, Tzvi is down the hall and out the door.

Jeremy looks slowly around the room at all the men swaying, their eyes focused on the leather-bound books in their hands. A man next to him scrunches his face and tosses his body, waist up, back and forth. Jeremy is impressed by this man's sense of balance.

Up front, Rabbi Norton calls out, *"Aleinu lishabe'ach..."*

"ALEINU LISHABE'ACH," a man shouts out from the side, pacing the length of the aisle, howling the words from his book with commanding gusto. He raises his face heavenwards and gestures broadly with his fist, miraculously missing the worshipers in his general proximity. "AL KEIN..."

Jeremy smiles and his eyes follow the man's journey back and forth, back and forth. Something of the words the man calls out is comforting and smoothly filling.

Next to him, the swayer closes his book and kisses it passionately. Jeremy regards this with mild shock. Kissing a book...you must admit, it's a bit odd.

The man, feeling Jeremy's gaze, glances up. His face breaks out in a half smile that seems almost apologetic, although the man has nothing to be apologetic about.

"Lem," the man says by way of introduction and hesitantly reaches out his hand. Jeremy doesn't think much of the whole shaking-hands deal, but Lem looks so delicate and sheepish, he'd hate to break the man's heart. Jeremy takes it fumblingly and gives it a nice tug, smiling encouragingly at him. A hand clamps firmly on his shoulder.

"Good Shabbos!" booms a voice behind him. "This your son, Lem?

"No... My son, he's younger, he..."

"Hey, don't worry about it. I'm not going to eat you. Right now, anyway."

Lem ducks his head down sheepishly and shoves his prayer book into a blue velvet bag.

"Kidding, hey, hey? Just kidding?"

"Of course, Dan. A good Shabbos to you and your family." Lem zips up the bag and darts around the table.

"Wait, wait, what's that — where are you going? You're eating with my family tonight, aren't you?"

"No, it's okay."

"It's not okay. The wife's expecting you!"

"I, I don't want to intrude or anything. I do have some food at my own house I could — "

"Don't make me tie you up and carry you to my house. End of topic. Now, are you going to introduce me to this young man here?"

"This young man is Jeremy," says Jeremy.

"A student?"

"Professor."

"Good to meet you. I'm a bit of a nuclear physicist myself. In my spare time. So, are you here for the rabbi?"

"Oh, I'm sorry, I thought this was the new sushi place. Well, I'll be going then..."

Dan leans his head back and lets out a deep roar of laughter.

"I like this one," he says to no one in particular. "Listen here, buddy. Because I like you, I'm going to give you a bit of worldly advice on the rabbi, yeah? See, Rabbi Norton, he's the best. But simple-minded. The kind that thinks everyone's an angel waiting to happen. We try not to burst his holy bubble."

"Um, Dan," says Lem.

"Hmm?"

"Maybe, let's not talk about Rabbi Norton like-"

"Ya, okay, okay. I'm just telling him to be careful what he says around him. Trying to protect my rabbi and stuff. I love the guy," he says to Jeremy, and Jeremy nods solemnly.

"Sorry," says Lem. "Sorry."

"No, you yell at me anytime you like, Lem Shlem. C'mon, let's get a move on for the meal. My wife made potato kugel; I tell you, the smell was bugging me all Friday. I can't wait to get myself a man-sized portion of that stuff. Jeremy." And he nods in Jeremy's general direction.

Lem tucks his velvet bag under his arm and trails Dan towards the exit.

"Nice meeting you," Lem calls over his shoulder, tossing Jeremy a rueful smile.

"Same here," Jeremy calls after him.

He jams his fists into his pockets and scuffs his shoe against a nearby chair leg, waiting for Rabbi Norton to notice him. Rabbi Norton is talking to someone in front of an embroidered curtain across the room.

Eventually, Rabbi Norton looks in his direction and his face lights up. He pats the shoulder of the man he's with and warmly wishes him a good Shabbos. Then he makes his way towards Jeremy, arms extended in greeting. Before Jeremy knows what has quite hit him, Rabbi Norton's hands are clamped on his shoulders and Rabbi Norton is looking straight into his eyes, beaming up at him.

"I'm so glad you could make it," he says in that soft, hushed voice of his that reminds Jeremy of the hum of an air-conditioning unit.

"Yeah, well, y'know. Nothing much else doing, with school not started yet and all. I figured I might as well."

"I'm so glad you did. I'm sorry I wasn't at home when you arrived. It's hard to estimate times with this community." Rabbi Norton chuckles good-humoredly as he steers Jeremy towards a crowded corner of the room. "Come. You'll want to meet Zev. You'll get along wonderfully. He wears nice ties."

Jeremy wonders why this would be sufficient reason for his liking someone, but as his gaze passes over the man in question, he can follow Rabbi Norton's line of reasoning.

A stout, paunchy man sits ensconced in an armchair, surrounded by a group of young black-hatted boys, the only differentiation between these boys seeming to be height. This said man is wearing a black tie with flying cows on it.

"Good Shabbos, Zev," greets Rabbi Norton.

"Good Shabbos, Moish," says Zev, smiling up at the rabbi. The boys echo Zev's greeting. Zev's gaze catches Jeremy's.

"Ah! Hello! I don't think we've met. Have we, Moish?"

"Hmmm?" Rabbi Norton appears distracted.

"Are you going to introduce me to this gentleman over here?"

"Oh," says Rabbi Norton. "Sorry, I was just thinking… I…if you'll excuse me, I must check if Lem is still here."

"No, he left," says Jeremy, but Rabbi Norton is already out of the shul room and down the hall.

"So…" says Zev.

"So so," says Jeremy. "Jeremy Briggs," and he salutes Zev.

Zev salutes back. "Zev Cohen," he says. "Nice to meet you. Love the hat."

"Love the tie," says Jeremy, fingering his striped New York Giants cap with a grin.

Zev looks proudly down at his cows. "Yeah, I love this one. Oh, these are my sons," and he stretches his short arm out wide and grins proudly at the sea of black surrounding him. "This is Yitzchak, my second oldest, and Menachem, Berel, Shmuli, Aaron… And this little one-" Zev punches the shoulder of a boy who looks to be about seven — "is Sruli."

"I'm not little," says Sruli with a frown.

Shmuli laughs, and Jeremy is pleasantly surprised to find some unexpected humor and personality. All the boys had seemed like clones to him.

Shmuli gets up and drags a chair near the wall into the huddle. "Sit," he says in a voice that brooks no conflict.

Jeremy plops himself down in a comfortable slouch, hands crossed behind his neck. "I'm starving," he says. "When do we eat?"

■ ■ ■

"Mike?"

Mike looks up in mild irritation from his laptop. He grunts. The door opens and Chad enters.

"Good evening, Michael," he says, making his way through a pile of papers and binders. He kicks a hole-puncher out of the way, a blizzard of confetti swirling about him. "Going to bed anytime soon?"

"No," says Mike, his fingers tapping busily at the keyboard.

"Well, you do know that college is starting in a couple days."

"Yes."

"Alright. I just thought I'd ask if you needed any school supplies, etcetera."

"No."

"Okay, then," says Chad. "Have yourself a good night...or whatever..."

"Hmmm. Mnnnn."

"I will. Oh, I forgot to mention that a friend of yours keeps calling."

Mike frowns.

"I'll get rid of him."

Mike nods. Suddenly he looks up, startled. Chad holds a pile of print-outs in his hand. "Put them down," Mike says.

"Oh...I'm sorry, I just thought I would freshen this room up a bit. Here they go. They're going right back down."

Mike watches Chad carefully.

"Good night, again," says Chad, backing out of the room. He closes the door behind him and inhales deeply.

Oxygen.

■ ■ ■

Jeremy declines to dance with the men as they sing *Shalom Aleichem*, choosing to be a passive bystander. When they sit down to sing *Eishes Chayil*, he steps forward to join them. It is then that he feels a tugging at his tee-shirt.

"Are you going to sit with us?" asks Tzvi, looking up at him expectantly.

Shmuli sends darting warning arrows with his eyes, but they bounce uselessly off Tzvi's obliviousness.

"Yeah, why not," says Jeremy, allowing himself to be led towards the children's end of the enormous dining room table.

"You're sitting here," Tzvi says.

"I want to sit on the other side," says Aaron.

"NO! I'm sitting there," says Sruli.

"No," says the girl with finality. "I ALWAYS sit there."

"Well, Jeremy's sitting in my seat, so I should get to-"

"Shhhh, shhhhhhh," says Tzvi, raising his pudgy hands for silence. "It's Shabbos. We're not supposed to fight, K? Rachel and Sruli can sit next to Jeremy, and then next time near me and Aaron. And Yanky doesn't even ever get a turn because we're all older than him."

"Yeah," says Rachel, giggling.

Aaron shrugs. Sruli happily plops himself down and wraps both arms around Jeremy's left bicep.

Next time? thinks Jeremy, but Rabbi Norton is already lifting an engraved silver cup in the air, calling out more mysterious words that curiously send shivers of both fear and excitement up and down his back. He wonders what it all means, and why Rabbi Norton cannot speak plain English like everybody else in the civilized world, yet at the same time it is all so beautiful and wonderful, and he wishes it would never stop — except that he is getting a tiny bit hungry.

■ ■ ■

Cream of chicken soup and potato kugel and cherry pie and little voices, mixed with the men's, bursting forth in a passionate chorus that seems to shake the very walls. Small chubby arms encircling his neck, his waist, his arms. Someone playing with his fingers; someone babbling in his ear would he like seconds; he must try the schnitzel; it's the best, the best, the best; and does he like the salad, 'cuz guess who helped make it.

■ ■ ■

As Jeremy leans back in his chair later that evening, with a snoring child curled up in his lap, he feels calmer than he's felt in weeks. It's as though he is sinking into a swirling of cotton stuffing, soft whispers, and a low-down, humming spring wrapping him in yellow-burgundy tenderness. It's as though he floats on air, encompassed in a warm surrounding. He closes his eyes, his stomach settled and comfortable from a well-cooked meal. Slowly, his eyelids weigh down as he finds that perfect place just outside of sleep and almost there, as his mind hangs on to a thread of this world, not quite slipped away but balanced in slightly pressing fuzz like a free fall.

Then he hears a voice calling to him from a distance, and he stretches himself outwards towards it.

He snaps his eyes open.

The room is empty, save for Rabbi Norton's face hovering above him. His lap seems empty and cold without the child's presence weighing down on it; the house is quiet, eerily so. His neck feels stiff and creaky.

"Whoa. Where are all the people?" he says, his mind still gauzy with fog.

"Sleeping. Zev and his family are in their apartment above the shul, and my family is upstairs. I should have woken you up sooner, but you looked so peaceful. I decided to learn just a little and then I learned a little bit more…

"Listen — it's late, it's dark. You're welcome to stay in our guest room for what's left of the night. I'm sure you're tired, and I'd feel better knowing you're here rather than walking around the streets at this hour."

Through the murkiness of his blurry thoughts, all Jeremy can gather is an invitation for sleep. He stumbles upstairs after Rabbi Norton, who pushes open a door just to the side of the landing.

"The washroom's right across the hall. There's a spare set of pajamas in the top drawer…" Rabbi Norton's voice trails off as Jeremy collapses spread-eagle on top of the blankets. "Nu, as long as you're comfortable."

Jeremy can hear Rabbi Norton talking, but the words are beyond the scope of his comprehension; white noise in a corner of his mind.

As he drifts off once more, a thought, a niggling little blip, passes through his consciousness…something he was supposed to do? But quick as it came, it is gone, making way for dreams and rest and blissful slumber.

Jeremy lets out a rousing snore as Rabbi Norton closes the door softly behind him.

"*Lailah tov*," he says to no one in particular.

CHAPTER 8
UNEXPECTED GUESTS

A perfect crease, a flipping of the hands, and a crisply folded shirt is laid neatly in Chad's suitcase.

He pinches the zipper tab with the ends of his thumb and forefinger, closing the suitcase in one fluid whooping sound. He hoists it out the door and into the hallway.

"Mike! I'm taking my luggage out to the car. Did you perchance pack anything you'd like me to take when I go?"

"Hallway."

"What? Oh, okay, I see it." See it? Yes, Chad saw it, a bright-red camp-connection duffel bag with misshapen bulges and a zipper that almost, but not quite, makes itself two-thirds closed against the strain of crammed, unfolded clothing.

Chad sighs and opens Mike's bag. He overturns it onto the floor and lowers himself down next to the pile, folding his legs beneath himself.

He can hear the blipping of Mike's Playstation 3 and the sound of some creature's strangled death throes. He rolls his eyes and folds a dark blue hoodie. He reaches for something else. His finger snaps against a hard surface. Wincing, he pulls at a buckled strap, revealing a laptop case. A strange expression crosses over his face. He opens it quickly and stares at the sleek object before him. He flips the lid and starts it up.

The Window's flag flaps merrily on the screen, and with a flash of blue and a swirling of white, the User Menu materializes.

Never before has he come across anything like it; the technology is incomparable to anything he has ever seen. The screen resolution is clearer than real life; the touch-pad responds like magic. After rummaging through the laptop case, Chad procures wireless ear buds that just require a small USB plug-in and some sort of remote-control glove.

"Wow," he whispers. He selects Mike's username. An alarm goes off in loud whoops, and the screen goes black, then bright purple and green. "NICE TRY, CHAD" appears in fluorescent orange letters.

"Stupid thing," says Chad, pounding random keys angrily, "stupid, stupid, stupid-"

"Nice."

Chad slams the laptop's lid down and turns to face Mike.

"Oh. Hi, Michael. I was just refolding some of your clothing." As he speaks, Chad snatches at socks and jeans, casually elbowing the laptop beneath the pile of clothes.

"No, you weren't."

Chad grins sheepishly and looks up at Mike. "Yes, okay, I wasn't. I was just examining that dandy piece of technology you've got here. Very nifty, if I do say so myself."

"Notebook."

"I beg your pardon?"

"It's called a notebook computer."

Chad waggles his index finger in an upward direction. "I knew that," he says.

"Yes. You did. And you weren't just examining it."

There is a long, awkward pause. Chad scratches his nose and inspects his fingernails, exploring his options, trying to think of what to say. Finally, he sighs and rests his forehead against the palm of his hand. "Fine, I wasn't."

Mike stands there and flicks his gaze across Chad's face.

"How long have you known?" asks Chad.

"Always. Since you started."

"You never told, you never said."

"I don't care."

"Oh. But then — can I check it out?"

Mike shakes his head curtly.

"What? Why not?"

Mike reaches down and picks up the notebook computer. He shuffles into his room and clicks the door behind him with finality.

"Suit yourself," Chad calls after him, grinding his teeth in frustration. He reaches into his pocket and pulls out a pad of paper and a pen. He scribbles something down. He knows it is not enough. Obviously. He will have to do better and do better fast.

■ ■ ■

"Jeremy...Jeremy...WAKE UP, JEREMY!"

Something pokes and jabs at his eyelid. Someone is by his feet, grunting in a pathetic attempt to move one of his legs.

"Jeremy!" the poker squawks. Jeremy lets out a rattling snore. Someone sighs.

"I'm going to tell Ima!" snaps Tzvi.

The children file out of the room. Jeremy watches them through his eyelashes.

The second they are out, he sits up quickly. He rubs his eyes fussily and lets out a jaw-cracking yawn. He stretches his arms out wide and bounds out of bed. He can't believe he actually spent the entire night hanging out at the rabbi's. He wonders what he missed last night on campus. Not that so many people are actually in yet, seeing as the semester doesn't start until Monday. He squints at the clock hanging across the room. Eleven on a Saturday? It's practically the middle of the night... From down the hall, he hears the clattering of little feet returning. Jeremy thinks fast.

"Jeremy," says Tzvi, standing with his hands on his hips, eyeing the blanket under which Jeremy's form is huddled, "please wake up."

"Jeremy," says Sruli, "Tzvi's mommy says if you don't get up right now, we can eat your *kiddush* cookies."

"JE-RE-MY…" whines Rachel, yanking furiously at one of her pigtails.

But Jeremy doesn't move.

"K fine," says Aaron, "you want Tzvi to tell his mommy? Fine, he'll tell her and then you're gonna-"

"BOOOOOOOOOOOO!!!!!" Jeremy bursts out of the closet to be met with four pairs of startled eyes. Rachel screeches and jumps several inches in the air. Sruli ducks in terror, and Aaron freezes in his spot.

Tzvi reaches beneath the covers of the bed and pulls out three arranged pillows, throwing them at Jeremy in succession.

"Ow," says Jeremy.

Tzvi isn't quite as amused as Jeremy expected. His eyebrows dip dangerously towards his nose and his bottom lip juts out, his chin tight.

"Whoa, whoa, whoa, buddy, it was just a joke, yeah?"

"Get dressed."

"Wha — these ARE my clothes."

Tzvi nods curtly. "So come," he says, and he stomps out of the room.

"That was kinda funny," says Sruli, latching on to Jeremy's hand and leading him downstairs.

"Yeah," says Aaron, "like when we were, 'Jeremy, you hafta get up!' and then — ROWR!!!!!!!!!"

"Yeah," says Sruli, and he cackles in pure glee.

"And Rachel was so, so, so, so, so SCARED."

"I was not."

"Were, too."

"And Tzvi was so, so, so, so scared too, didja see?" and the two boys collapse on the stairs in delighted laughter.

Jeremy smirks down at them, then skips over their forms and drops down the remaining stairs.

"Tzvi," he calls out, chasing his receding figure. Tzvi turns back and regards Jeremy warily.

"Hey, buddy, I thought it would be pretty funny. I didn't mean to scare ya."

Tzvi shrugs and kicks at the hallway baseboard. "I wasn't scared," he says, "at least not so much."

Jeremy chuckles and crouches down to Tzvi's height. "I'm sorry," he says and holds out his arms. Tzvi looks at him in confusion. Jeremy laughs. He walks over to Tzvi and swoops him up into a giant bear hug.

"So, what's this *kiddush* stuff you were talking about?" he asks.

"That way." Tzvi points towards the kitchen.

By the time the men and boys are home from shul, Jeremy is comfortably situated in a kitchen chair with a child on each knee, a pile of cookie crumbs on the table before him.

"Hey! Anything left for a poor starving boy?" asks Shmuli, sitting down next to Jeremy.

Rabbi Norton looks up from the *sefer* he's been walking around with, and his eyes settle on Jeremy.

"Aha! Jeremy, good to see you're still here. Will you be joining us for lunch?"

Jeremy scrunches his face up apologetically and shakes his head.

"Naaaw," he says. "I gotta get back to the school."

"No, Jeremy! Stay!" screams Sruli, launching himself onto Shmuli's lap and throwing his arms around Jeremy's neck.

"What — you want me to stay? That what you trying to say, Sruli? Are you holding me captive?"

"Yep," says Sruli, grinning a close-mouthed grin, smug as an apple.

"Not going to let me go?"

"No," says Rachel, stomping her foot in finality. "Stay here."

"You're gonna miss my mother's potato kugel," warns Shmuli.

"Yeah, Mrs. Cohen's potato kugel is the best!" says Tzvi, then ducks his head as Mrs. Norton coughs.

"Also, you can't leave, 'cuz I'm just gonna lock the door and then you're gonna HAVE to stay." Aaron folds his arms stubbornly.

"Alright, alright, alright, since you all asked so nicely," says Jeremy, smiling as he gently pries Sruli's fingers off his neck. He holds up his hands in mock surrender.

"Yay, yay, Jeremy's gonna stay, stay, stay!" Sruli screams at the top of his lungs. Rachel does a little twirly skip-dance in place, and Tzvi snuggles closer to Jeremy's chest. Jeremy smiles and closes his eyes, wondering if all this can be real, this perfect, perfect, wonderful world.

By the time Jeremy leaves Rabbi Norton's house later that afternoon, he feels as though he is leaving home, as though the further he walks from the house, the more it pulls at him, like he's attached to it by elastic string.

His ears ring with the thumping of fists on hardwood table and the resounding chorus of voices soaring upwards in a joyful harmony of, "*Yonah, yonah matza....*"

His heart is filled with a sense of stillness, and he hums a tuneless little tune as he heads into his dorm.

He waves obligingly at all the eager greetings, flashing three-fingered salutes at random intervals and "hey, how's it goin'" and bopping passing science majors fondly on the head like the mole in the hole. In this manner, he is able to make his way all the way to the comforting realm of his dorm room.

Thankful that he has managed to arrive safely, he collapses onto his bed, folding his arms behind his neck and beaming up at the ceiling.

The door slams open with a bang, and there is Cole, snapping his knuckles one at a time as he stands rigid in the doorway.

"Jay," he says, cracking his scrawny neck with a jerk of his head.

"Oh. Hi, Cole, how's it going?"

"You weren't there last night."

Realization rushes into the pit of Jeremy's stomach. "Right," he says. "Sorry about that."

"Sorry isn't what I'm looking for."

"What is?"

"Huh?"

"What are you looking for, then?"

Cole lifts his index finger and jabs it threateningly at Jeremy. "Tonight you better be there." His voice is low and menacing. His unibrow is scrunched. His Mohawk bristles as he turns on his Doc Marten heels and stalks off. Jeremy throws a tissue at his receding back.

In his head, Jeremy can faintly hear Mike's sardonic voice asking him, "Why do you hang out with him, anyway? There are plenty of happier people where he came from."

Jeremy rolls onto his side and stares at the empty bed across from his. "Because I want to," he whispers, then moans and slams his pillow on top of his head. A few seconds later he takes it off and sits up, slinging his feet over the edge of his bed.

"Hey, Sam, close the door for me, will you?" he calls at a passing student.

"Oh, sure, no problem," Sam says and does so, stunned Jeremy knew his name.

Jeremy slumps back onto bed and tries to recapture the bliss he'd been feeling minutes before. "*Yonah, yonah matza...*" he sings to himself and an awkward smile creeps back onto his face.

Master Briggs was not one to hold his self-worth by the thoughts and opinions of the common peasantry. Although, being a landowner, he had much need for their presence, this said presence was merely tolerated. But soon would come the day when he could finally settle his accounts and rid his lands of their coarse ways and customs. Yes, one day these porcine beings would find out just what sort of man Master Briggs was. Those who sought to place their power above his would find themselves left behind, whimpering in his shadows, as he stood tall above all other men. The world would know his name. The world would be in awe of it.

■ ■ ■

"Hello? Is anybody home?" Shelly opens the screen door a crack. "Hello?"

"One second..." Minna rushes to the door, wiping the palms of her hands on her apron. "Oh, Shelly, how are you?"

"Amazing. And you?"

"*Baruch* Hashem, everything is wonderful. Come in, come in." Minna shepherds her inwards towards the living room. "Sit down. Can I get you anything?"

"No, I'm fine. I'm just here because I think I might have left my purse here last time I came."

"Dark purple?"

"Yes, that's it."

"Oh, I put it somewhere. Hang on while I go look for it. Make yourself at home."

"Totally." Shelly looks around the room. Make herself at home? The Nortons' house always feels like home to her.

Like the home she never had.

Her favorite part of it are the picture frames that practically wallpaper the walls, face after smiling face, braces to straightened teeth...the journey to adulthood. There is Rabbi Norton's eldest son at his wedding...Minna beaming with baby Tzvi in her arms...

their only daughter at her eighth grade graduation…the twins, twelve years old, a picture they sent of themselves in yeshiva…so many smiling faces. Instinctively, Shelly smiles back.

"This picture always makes me laugh."

Shelly turns around, curling a stray piece of hair around her ear. "Which one?"

"Of those two rascals." Minna walks up to Shelly and points to the picture of the twins. "They look so innocent here, but if you look closely… see? Chezzy's tickling Yosef."

"Omigosh! I totally didn't notice that!"

Minna titters and plunks Shelly's bag down on the coffee table.

Shelly clenches her fists and hesitantly clears her throat. Now or never. "Minna?" she says quietly.

"Yes?" Minna leans over the corner table and straightens out some *tchatchkes*.

"Can I ask you something? Like, something kind of personal?"

"Of course you can, *mammelah*."

Minna sits down on the couch and looks up at Shelly seriously. Shelly sits down next to her and takes a deep breath before forging onwards. She doesn't let herself think too much, because then she knows she will be too embarrassed to ask.

"It's just something I'm not getting. Like, why do you do this? This whole deal with, you know, inviting people to your house, teaching them all about the Torah and *mitzvot*. I mean, you're totally living in the middle of nowhere, without your kids, and, like, basically there's no one else like you here, if you know what I'm saying? Like, is it worth it?"

Minna smiles a quiet little smile and folds her hands neatly over her crossed legs. An air of calm, sweet satisfaction envelopes her, reaching out to touch the edges of Shelly's perception. "You know," she says, "it's so funny, because I was thinking something similar the other day. Yosef called home, 'just to talk,' he said, but I could tell he was homesick. And I thought to myself: Maybe it is the wrong thing. Is it not the first job of a Jewish mother to be there for her children? And then I thought: But I AM there for my children. Years ago in Europe, a *yiddishe mammeh* used to send her little boy off to yeshiva so young and not hear from him for years. And still, her children knew that she was there for them. My situation is very much like that. Yes, sometimes it gets lonely for me here, and I do miss my children terribly, but really, they're just a couple hours' drive away. Is it worth the separation? Of course it is."

"For what? Like, why…"

"Why did I decide to do this? Truth is, I didn't. It was my husband's decision. Spur of the moment. One day, he just came home from *kollel* all excited because he made up his mind. He makes his important decisions very suddenly, my husband… Like when he decided to become religious. He wasn't always religious, you know."

"No way. The rabbi?!"

"He was a real hippie growing up. Long hair, peace, love, and brotherhood…the works. When he was in university about thirty years back, majoring in the arts, he met a rabbi who invited him over for a Shabbos…and so the story goes." Minna smiles to herself. "Now, he just wants to do the same."

"So THAT'S why he made you leave, like, everything?! He totally just dragged you away from your life to-"

"No, Shelly. He didn't make me do anything. Had I not wanted to go, he never would have made me. Truth was, at the time, I was so scared, but I wanted to do what my husband wanted. And I'm glad I did."

"Why?"

"Oh, so many reasons. I'm happy."

"But you never have time for yourself! Like, your house is like a hotel, for goodness' sake!"

"And I love it. I wouldn't have it any other way. It's a wonderful feeling, not to be so self-absorbed. Once I realized that this world is not only about my own needs, it's almost like a load was taken off my shoulders. Giving to others, sharing with others, it's like the joy of my life is being multiplied over and over again with the amount that I can do. I'm so happy. Happier than I was living in the city with all my friends and family. I'm fulfilled."

"Oh. I guess I was just kind of wondering if people like me were a burden-"

"Never! *Chas v'shalom!*"

"What you said about how it's easier when it's not always about you…that's, like, I don't know if I get it…"

"You will."

"I hope. But you know, Minna, you and your husband…you really are the happiest people I know, so I guess you know what you're talking about. I'm sorry if I was nosy, like if I offended you or anything…"

"Not at all, not at all. You know me better than that, Shelly."

Shelly giggles, biting her lip. "Yeah... Anyway, I'm totally rushing out on you all of a sudden, but I've got to be somewhere, like, in five minutes."

"Hold on, I'll walk you to the door." Minna gets up from the couch and they exit the living room, Minna flicking the light off as they leave. "Will I be seeing you again sometime soon?"

"I dunno..."

"How about this Shabbos?"

"Actually, I might be going to Israel again in a couple days."

"Wow, really?!"

"I'm not sure yet. We'll see... I'll call you."

"Alright, Shelly. Good to see you."

"Great seeing you, too! Bye, Rebbetzin!"

Shelly waves and heads across the lawn to her shiny purple car. As she opens the door, an old van belches down the road towards her, parking across the road. Frumma flounces out of the driver's seat, yelling at her daughter to stay near the car because it's only going to be a small stop. "Hello, Shelly!" she yodels as she passes her on the way to the house. Shelly waves.

"Hi!" It's Rachel, tugging at her jeans.

"Hi, Rachel! Good to see you again. Nice dress!"

Rachel smiles and smoothes out the rumpled, pink polka-dotted material. "I hate it when my mommy goes to Mrs. Norton's house. She always takes so long."

"How about you play with Tzvi?"

"Tzvi is too wild," she says, stomping her feet, "and he always wants to play baseball. It's not fun with only two people. Is this your car?"

"Yes, it is. Actually, I'm leaving right now."

"Ooooooooh..." Rachel stands back from the car as Shelly gets into the driver's seat. Just as she straps on her seatbelt, Rachel leans in through the window and pecks her gently on her cheek.

"Aaaaw...Rachel! What was that for?"

"Because you look sad. Don't be sad, Shelly."

"No...Shelly's just...a little bit nervous about things."

"How come?"

"Because Shelly's a big girl now, and she has to make big-girl decisions that are very important."

"Ooooooooh..." Rachel's eyes grow very big. "But don't be sad. K?"

"Okay. Bye now, Rachel."

"Bye!"

As Shelly pulls away from the curb and heads towards the stop sign, she finds herself biting back the sobs that threaten to overwhelm her. Don't be sad? Don't be sad? Not sad... Hopeless. That's it. She feels so hopeless.

She parks the car after she turns the corner and presses her face into the steering wheel. "I don't know what to do. I don't know what to do," she wails, sobs wrenching her shoulders up and down as waves of despair pull at the back of her eyes and the tips of her finger and toes. "G-d, I don't know what to do. I just don't know what to do."

CHAPTER 9
SO LONG AND HELLO

Mike leaves the house around ten a.m. that morning, hitching a ride with some random university students who knew him from last year.

Chad, however, stays home, pacing the hardwood floor of his bedroom in crisp footfalls. He clasps his hands together behind his back, and as he does so, he wonders what university life will be like. He remembers hearing from someone sometime that, with Mike in his first year there, it was endless partying and racing go-karts in the parking lot and swimming in the fountain. But Mike always had had those sort of weird ideas... Things like that never happen to him; he always seems to be left at the sidelines when it comes to the people Mike hangs out with. However, the university being as big as it is, there is no doubt in his mind that he will soon find the perfect group of associates and participate in all sorts of mind-opening and rip-roaring experiences.

A slight smile slides across his face. He can't wait to introduce himself to Professor Carl, a good friend of Uncle Rob's and the man who pulled the strings to get Chad into MBU.

Chad thinks about the upcoming year, about the new doors of knowledge that will soon be opening up for him; his heart flutters in anticipation of the many things he will learn.

He tries to imagine how the grounds will look during a school day, streaming with students.

He wonders if there will be a chess team.

And then it is time to get into his father's Jaguar, and then they head fifteen minutes outside of the city to a "campus isolated from the stress and hustle of the city, where students can thrive in a peaceful atmosphere and reach their full potential."

Sitting in the back seat of the car, sandwiched between duffel bags, staring at the graying back of his father's head, Chad flicks imaginary dirt off his pants. He rehearses over in his mind a few lines of introduction. He scratches his nose.

The car pulls into the parking lot right outside Chad's dorm. Ben hops out of the driver's seat and goes around to the back. Chad joins him there. Ben yanks out one of Chad's duffel bags, the veins on the back of his neck protruding against the outside of his skin as the strap digs into the backs of his fingers.

Chad makes a move to take the other strap, but Ben turns a shoulder away from him.

"Careful, Dad. You don't want to strain your back now."

A stubborn scowl pulls at the edges of Ben's mouth. "It'll take more than a puny little piece of luggage to take me down," he mutters to himself. With one great heave, he settles the bag on his back and staggers in an unsteady, lopsided path toward the dorm doors.

"See?" he wheezes. "Piece of cake. Hardly weighs anything."

Chad sighs. "Have it your way, Dad," he says and turns back to the trunk. His mother has joined him there, and she helps him hoist out the next piece of luggage.

Chad easily swings the strap over his shoulder and reaches once more into the trunk. With a spring in his step, he heads into the building, suitcases hanging from his shoulders and knuckles. He passes his father coming up the stairs. Ben pretends not to notice. Chad smiles in satisfaction as he breezes into his dorm room.

His father is seated comfortably in the driver's seat when Chad returns to the car once more. The keys are in the ignition and the radio buzzes and squeaks a blow-by-blow account of a soccer game.

Standing by the passenger door, Claire winds her wedding ring around and around her finger.

"You be good now, Chad. Take care of your brother. Don't, don't forget to eat."

"Sure thing, Mother," says Chad. He tries to meet his mother's eyes, but she is staring off into the distance, blinking rapidly.

"Hey, c'mon, Mother. I'll be back home for winter vacation. It's not so long."

"Oh, phooey, I know that," says Claire, managing a wobbly smile. She places a hand on Chad's shoulder and stands on tiptoe to give him a quick peck on the cheek.

Chad grins and throws his arms around her, lifting her up in the air in a tight embrace.

"Put me right back down, you cheeky scoundrel," says Claire. She adjusts her sunglasses more firmly into her hair and sniffs, nose in the air, hiding her glow of pleasure.

"Love you, Mother."

Claire nods. "Love you, too, Chad. Goodbye now." And she opens the passenger door of the car, settling herself in and buckling up.

Chad makes his way around to the driver's side.

"Bye, Dad," he says, sticking out his hand. "Drive safe."

"Hmmm," says Ben. He looks up from the steering wheel and takes Chad's hand, strangling it in a manly handshake. "Ah, Chad. You'll be calling in a week, begging to come home, missing your mummy."

"Love you, too, Dad," Chad says, rolling his eyes.

He steps away from the car and waves good-naturedly at his mother's face turned anxiously toward the back window as the car pulls away until it is beyond his range of vision.

Then Chad is on his own.

He squares his shoulders and struts his way to the center lawn for registration.

He finds the table for business and political science manned by a second-year student with a Crest White-strip smile and a way of swiveling his head around in curiosity like a skinny owl with good dental care.

"Hi," says Chad, reaching a hand out across the table. "Chad Burns."

The Crest owl nudges a boy sitting hunched over the table. The boy looks up from the textbook he'd been engrossed in, his eyeballs pricking in suspicion.

"Greetings," he says.

"Chad Burns," says Chad again.

The owl checks his name off on a clipboard.

The other hands Chad a tag and a package. "You may purchase all supplies at the bookstore prior to the west wing of the Harold-Smithonian Memorial Library."

"Why, thank you. I shall do just that," says Chad. He walks off towards a towering pink stone building near the center of the campus. Suddenly, he stops. He turns quickly on the back of his left dress shoe and heads back towards the table in hurried steps.

The owl is busy with another student. The other boy is back in the world of his Popular Physics textbook.

"Hello, again," says Chad. The boy looks up and regards him oddly.

"I'm sorry for disturbing you, but I do believe you failed to introduce yourself."

"Pardon?"

"Your name…?"

"Oh." The boy looks shocked. He closes his textbook with a snap and reaches for Chad's outstretched hand.

Chad grasps it firmly and smiles at the boy encouragingly.

"Saul Rotter. Pleased to make your acquaintance."

"Same here." Chad beams at Saul as he backs away from him, waving. A flicker of horror crosses Saul's face. Next thing Chad knows, he is hit by a brick wall and the world is crashing down on him. The sky is spinning, and an ugly, leering face attached to a spindly neck is glaring down at him.

"Hey, loser, watch where you're going."

"I beg your pardon," says Chad, sitting up groggily, watching the world ooze past him in swirls. He stumbles to his feet and sparkles a grin back at this boy's lip ring.

"Loser," says the boy.

"I say, but those are some tough stomach muscles you've got there." Chad winces as he rubs the back of his head.

Cole snorts like a horse and lifts his shirt to display a bulletproof vest. "Loser," he says again, and shoves Chad back down before stomping off.

"Friendly," Chad remarks.

Saul shrugs and returns to his Popular Physics.

Chad frowns and slaps at the dust marks on his pants.

■ ■ ■

As Jeremy lugs his backpack of equipment down the dorm hallway, his ears are met with screams and explosions. His head perks up and he stares at his door, his eyes popping wide.

"Mike!" Jeremy howls, bursting into the dorm room.

Two overflowing duffel bags are left calmly parked on a bare mattress where Chad left them. Mike sits in front of a carefully unpacked and set-up monitor, remote gun in hand, blasting green toad-creatures into slime puddles with meticulous precision.

"When did you get in?"

"Before."

"Well, yeah. I was out all morning getting all my stuff for school. You did that yet? ...Mike, did you get your textbooks yet?"

"No."

"True. I mean, it's not like you ever use them or anything."

Mike reaches to his left without looking up from the monitor. He waves another gun at Jeremy.

"Naaw." Jeremy turns down the offer. "Cole's got something going on in his space, and I'm crashing."

Jeremy waits for the response that he knows is coming. Mike does not disappoint him. "Why are you still hanging out with that numbskull?"

"Why do I hang out with you? We're friends."

Mike shrugs. "Are we friends?" There is a slight tilt in his toneless voice that turns the concept of friendship into a juvenile concept not worthy of his passing interest.

Jeremy regards Mike's hunched figure with amused delight. Mike hears Jeremy walk to his dresser and rummage through a drawer. He returns to him shortly.

"It's good to have you back, buddy," Jeremy says and jams his watermelon cap down on top of Mike's hooded head. Chuckling to himself, he leaves the room. Mike reaches up and turns the rim of the cap out of his line of vision. He lifts his right hand and kills three frogs.

CHAPTER 10
SLIGHT CHANCE OF SHOWERS

It's the first day of school. He meant to go, but...things came up.

Such as sleep.

He groans and rolls over in bed, pulling his alarm clock from his shelf for a closer look. Eleven?! Why did he wake up?

He reaches below his pillow for his cell phone. Six missed calls. Oh. That's why.

New text message: *Go out rite now, it's da best! From #1 uncle in the world.*

Mike rolls his eyes. What time did it come? Ten-thirty...

Great.

The phone rings again, flashing blue. "Alright," mutters Mike, "I'm coming."

He yanks on a pair of jeans and a hoodie over

his PJs and shoves his feet into his Converse All Stars, crushing their already-smashed backings as he does so.

Outside the door of his dorm is a muscular guy who is leaning casually against a shiny tow truck. "Hey, kid," he drawls, "can you find Mike Burns for me?"

Mike shrugs. "What do you want?"

"What?" says muscle-guy, yanking off his sunglasses and scratching behind his ears.

"I'm Mike. What do you want?"

The man laughs loudly. "Oh, I get it. You're the one that kept me waitin' all this time."

Mike takes a step backwards.

The guy shrugs. He whips out a clipboard from nowhere. "Awright... I'm gonna hafta have some sorta codeword before-"

"Fuzzy Hamster." Mike glares at the sidewalk.

"Weyeeeeeeeeeeeell. You're definitely the guy, so..." — he widens his arms for dramatic effect — "that there beauty's for you. Your uncle says it's a replacement for last year's, whatever happened. That's all he told me to say, K? Lucky kid, that there vee-hicle is thoroughbred Lamborghini material." And he gestures to the shiny cherry-red car attached to his truck cable.

Mike allows himself a small smile. Nice.

"So I just need you to sign this here paper — yeah, right over there — and then I'm gonna let the car down right here, and...oh, this is for you." He dangles the keys at Mike. Mike swipes them away from him and begins to turn back.

The guy hops into the front of his truck to let the car down. It is then that Mike feels a familiar presence at his back.

"My goodness," says Chad. "That is a really sleek automobile, if I do say so myself."

Mike turns to him, a question flickering across his brow.

"Uncle Rob called me when he couldn't get through to you… Slept in?"

Mike shrugs.

Chad looks around, frowning slightly. "And where's mine?"

Mike waves the keys in front of Chad's face.

Chad cheers up. "Yes, you are definitely correct. There is no way Mother will let you have this car once she finds out. It's as good as mine."

"Not yet."

"Oh, have faith, Mike, I would never tell her. But…seeing as I didn't get one of my own, could I…?"

Mike bites his bottom lip. "Ask me first."

"Fair enough. Well," Chad says, patting Mike on the back, "I'm glad you came out on your own, and, well, you enjoy it…for now, har har. I've got to run back to class; I shouldn't even have left."

Mike nods. He feels quieted and calm as he watches Chad strut off. He handled that situation very well, if he may say so himself.

He always knows how to talk to Chad.

It's a comfort to be able to predict how someone will react, and then act accordingly. He seems to only be able to do this with his family and Jeremy. It gives him a secure and "right" feeling, because he knows he will always be able to rely on them to be themselves. They don't change. They didn't, not even when...he did.

∎ ∎ ∎

"Gordon?"

"Hmm?" Gordon doesn't look up from the stack of papers piled up on his keyboard. He squints, jabbing his nose closer to what he's reading as his brow furrows in concentration.

Ben sighs and enters the office, letting the door click quietly shut behind him.

"Have you seen the latest report on the LaserQuim?"

"Looking at it right now, actually."

"Oh. I'll give you a moment, then."

"Everything looks pretty great so far, though."

"Really? Okay."

"Did you want to tell me something, Ben?"

"It's nothing, really."

"Don't do that."

"I.... I just happened to notice a slight drop."

"Yes, that happens day to day, hour to hour... Little drops don't mean much on a constant rise. You know that."

"Of course I do."

Gordon straightens the papers, giving each side of the stack a few bangs on the edge of his desk.

"What is it, then?" he asks, looking up at Ben, eyebrows triangulated in desperate stress.

"It's...Gordon, there's a reason for this drop. I checked it out extensively."

"Ben, just say it."

"MaxCom is coming out with its own version of LaserQuim. It's not as high-quality, naturally, but it's cheaper."

Gordon spins his chair around to face his wall-sized window. He rests his chin on twined fingers and mutters in a hauntingly depressed tone of voice, "MaxCom strikes again."

"Big surprise."

"I almost expected this, you know?"

"I did expect it. That's why I checked."

"What are we going to do now, Ben?"

"It's not the end of the world just yet. Let's just...breathe...alright?

"NO! No, there's no time to breathe. It IS the end of the world, Ben; this is a huge deal! Think. Just THINK. First time Maxcom came out with our thing, I figured, well, maybe both companies were working on the same thing at the same time — coincidence, right? Second time around, they came out with a copy three months after us. So they're low-minded, monkey-ing losers. But still, no problem making a copy in three months. Next, it took a month. Still possible, maybe, working around a twenty-four-hour clock. But this is ridiculous. Our version has only been out three weeks! There's no way they could have done this without knowing about it way before it came out."

"It's impossible that they could have known about it, though," Ben counters. "The only ones who knew exactly where we were going with this was the guy who came up with the whole LaserQuim idea, and he would never tell, and then there's only you, me, and...Rob."

"Precisely." Gordon's eyes narrow into snake-like slits.

"Gordon?" Ben turns his head sideways, regarding Gordon's back in curiosity.

"Yes?"

Ben's eyes snap open as he stands in shock, as though he'd just been slapped in the face. "Oh, is that how it's going to be? We're going to go on a mole-hunt? Goodbye to companionship, trust, peace. No, now it's war, trying to oust somebody who probably doesn't even EXIST outside your paranoid melodramatic puny little.... ??!!"

"Oh, you don't think the mole exists then, Burns?" Gordon's voice slyly teases.

Ben grinds his teeth and sets his chin firmly. "Quite to the contrary, I know it does."

Gordon spins his chair back in a swift, sharp motion. He shifts his presence across the desk threateningly.

"I'm sure we will find out who it is in due time," he says in a creepily amiable tone. *Don't play games with me, Ben,* his eyes say in hardened coldness.

"Yes, I'm certain that we will." *I never said it was a game. On the contrary.*

A ding pierces the biting tension. "Message for*: Mr. Gordon* from*: Rob.*"

Gordon growls under his breath and his veins strain against his temples.

"I'll...get that," says Ben in exasperation. He walks up to the communication console and clicks the green button.

The room glows blue and then Rob's face appears on the wall before them.

"Hey!" Rob says, his face beaming in delight. "Gordon?"

"Yes, sir?" Gordon grits out.

"Have you seen — BEN! There you are! See, I was trying to reach you, but you're not in your office."

"Nope, evidently not," says Ben.

"Yeah, I figured you'd be with Gordon or something."

"Great, brilliant. What can I help you with today, Rob? You want me to come up there?"

"Naaw, that's alright. I just wanted to tell you that Rob, yes, me, Rob, Rob the Great, Rob the Mighty, has officially gotten to the next mission in BladeCraft!!!"

"Congratulations."

"I knew you'd say that," says Rob, chortling.

"Um, but Rob, while you're up there, there's something Gordon and I have discovered."

"Hmm?"

"It's about a mole from Maxcom."

"Of course — That! ...Gordon picked up on it? No way. I didn't figure that he could, though you, Ben, of course would do it. But you must admit — it's brilliant."

"Is it?" says Ben, suddenly feeling very tired.

"Yes, it's amazing! It's the best! I'm so glad you both figured it out; now you see how delightfully delightful this all is!"

Gordon sputters behind Ben's back.

"Oh, I'm so sorry, Gordon. I didn't mean to insult you just before about not picking up on it...Well, gotta go. Keep it up, you two."

And then he bleeps off.

"He's an IDIOT! He's a complete AIRHEAD!" Gordon fills his cheeks with air and then slowly lets it out through puckered lips. Then he sighs and slumps down into his leather swivel chair.

An awkwardness has replaced the formerly charged atmosphere in the room, and Ben and Gordon eye each other.

"I...you sure you want to go ahead with this whole 'find the traitor' thing, Gordon?"

"Naturally. After all, you heard it from Rob himself — it's brilliant. He...or she...yeah, we're going to find out who it is, and then we're going to do SOMETHING. We're going to make an example of this one, for all the world to see."

"Alright, have it your way. But you know, as a side point, Rob is not an idiot."

Gordon bobs his head in thought. "No, you're right, he's not. He most certainly isn't... But he's still an airhead."

Ben eyes Gordon for a moment. "So where do we start with the search?"

"With department reports and a list of workers, naturally..."

Ben cuts him off. "That won't get us anywhere."

"It's a start."

"Have it your way. But I may be busy this week and all. I don't know how much you can count on me for help with this."

"Busy?" Gordon's left eyebrow lifts slightly.

"Afraid so." Ben stands at the open door, hand on the post, ready to leave. "Don't spend too much time on this, alright? Good day." *This isn't over yet*, are the unspoken words that hang between them.

"Good day to you, too," says Gordon, nodding curtly at the closing door.

■ ■ ■

Jeremy feels his eyelids droop as he lies face-up on his bed, the clicking of Mike's keyboard making for a hypnotic undertone in the background.

Cold, slushy rain splatters against the dorm room window. A laundry bag filled with Mike's clean clothes clings wearily to the closet knob where Chad left it that morning. An overturned cardboard box lies between the two beds with 'Coffee Table' scrawled on it in black magic marker. A monitor stares blankly at the room's occupants, with Jeremy's boom box sitting next to it, keeping it squalid company.

Jeremy rolls onto his stomach with a sigh. The red letters on his bedside clock read 2:57 a.m. Mike has a class 7:30 in the morning, but he doesn't seem overly concerned.

"Jamie was asking about you," Jeremy says, drowsiness tugging at his voice.

Mike shrugs carelessly, not pausing in his clicking.

Jeremy shakes his head, feeling slightly frustrated at Mike's attitude. He is shocked by this feeling; what is he, Mike's mom? But he can't help himself.

"You've been on that computer all day for the past month. You didn't come to the beginning of the year bash. You haven't done anything since you came here, actually… What happened with surfing down the library stairs and stuff? All of a sudden, you're like Papa Gloom. I can't believe you haven't been out. People are asking me if you even came up to the school yet."

Mike doesn't respond, but Jeremy knows he's listening.

"I mean, I'm not your dad or anything, I was just," and Jeremy lets out a floor-shaking yawn, "s'cuse me…I was just wondering what's up with it all. Some sort of phase?"

"Phase?" Mike echoes, and he looks up from his laptop.

"Wrong word?"

"It's not a phase."

Jeremy snorts and hugs his pillow to his chest, sending the ceiling a conspiratorial, can-you-believe-this-person glance. "Everybody goes through phases. Get over yourself."

"A phase passes."

"Okay…" Jeremy regards Mike's hunched figure in amusement. "You saying you're going to be like this forever? Shrunken old grandpa still grunting around in hoodies? That what you're saying?"

"I don't know," says Mike, and, quite unexpectedly, his voice seems to catch.

Jeremy sits up and looks over at Mike, his smile gone now. "Mike buddy, you all right?"

Mike slams his laptop shut and rests his head on top of it. "Not really," he mumbles.

Jeremy's mouth forms as though he is saying "ooh," although no sound comes out. He then seems to wince, tugging at the bottom of his ragged tee. "Well, um," and he clears his throat uncomfortably, "anything you need to say, you know, just, go ahead…"

Mike doesn't look at him as he speaks. It is as though he is talking to the walls of the room, and his voice is a muted monotone. "I guess this is all because I thought. Whenever I think, I mess things up… Everything goes wrong."

"Naaw. You're a brilliant guy, Mike. Nothing wrong with you thinking."

"There's everything wrong with it. I shouldn't think so much. But I did. I was on the cliff line watching sunrise, last time we went. It was right after exams last year…do you remember?"

"Like I could forget it if I wanted to," says Jeremy, smiling anxiously at the memory.

"Well…that's when it all began. This line of thought, I mean. I thought about the world and what it was all supposed to be about and how nothing made sense — and then I couldn't be that crazy Mike kid anymore. The hyper-ness was gone. Who cares if I'm crazy, who cares if I make my mark on the world, you know? So what? One of these days I'm going to die, and everyone will die, and it just keeps going like that — you live and then you die. You're gone. You fade into nothingness. It's like you never were, you never felt, never wanted, never breathed. And if so, why bother?

"And then I got to thinking more. People need a purpose in this world. Some of them, they make money, some are famous... The happiest people who I know are the ones with children. With children, you kind of continue after death. Maybe that's why parents try to live through their children. But no point in that. Your children are going to be gone in the next few decades or so, too. You have grandchildren, but they'll die, too; they'll all die, and each person in their life will be trying so hard. They'll cry over disappointments and stress over life's details, and they'll be stupid for it, because it makes no difference. They're still going to be gone soon. They're just part of a life that was made by a freak accident. We're all a mistake not meant to be, and we're better off not being here.

"It's all so purposeless. People get so caught up in the nothingness...what are they accomplishing? Why bother? Suddenly there was this big emptiness inside me. I feel like I'm the only one who gets it. I despise people who make such big deals over issues — nothing is a big deal. They're nothing. And they don't even get it.

"But at the same time, I know that there's something wrong with that conclusion. I mean, there's got to be an answer somewhere... It can't be that this is all just a fluke.

"It's not a phase; it's my whole life, it's everything. Just because I'm younger doesn't mean I'm a child, you know? It's not some immature problem. And I don't want to be like this forever, with these thoughts circling in my head, but nobody's going to be breaking the cycle..."

Mike looks off to the side, his eyes distant. Jeremy is stunned. It is a lot to digest. Too much, he thinks, for a kid Mike's age.

What Mike had done last time at the cliff line...it starts to make a little bit of sense. Such an unsettling line of thinking begins to get even him anxious. He has no answers for Mike. He feels compelled, though, to respond.

"Break the cycle. Huh. Well, that's a toughie...I haven't thought much about this concept... I dunno that I have the answers."

"No, I didn't think so." Mike re-opens his laptop and stares at the screen.

"It's like, I'm not sure I'm understanding exactly everything you're saying."

"I don't care whether you understand or not." Mike's voice gives away his sad defeat.

"Wait, wait, I don't mean that I don't understand. I'm just...I'm twenty-three, man. I'm not some guru person..."

Mike is gone, and Jeremy chews his lip, blinking vigorously at the floor as he struggles to find the right words to draw Mike back out of his shell. Desperation grips him; perhaps he lost his chance. He sends a quick prayer heavenward before speaking again.

"I know this guy, right? Holy and stuff. I've been hanging around him a lot lately, just talking and all. I swear he's got these answers; he can tell you what you want to know."

Mike looks up. "Holy?"

"Yeah, his name's Rabbi Norton."

"Rabbi? Religion? That's your answer?" Mike's voice is cynically aloof.

"Hey, you ARE Jewish, right? He's Jewish, you're Jewish...why not? Might be interesting. Come with me next time I go. We're actually having this question and answer thing. Can't hurt."

Mike shrugs.

■ ■ ■

At five o'clock, Jeremy returns from Visual Arts III to the usual comforting snores coming from Mike's side of the room. A smile breaks across his face as his gaze passes over the tie he just purchased, maroon with smiley faces, which lies thrown over the foot of his bed where he left it.

"Mike," he says with practiced patience to the sleeping figure huddled under the tangled sheets, "get up! We have to leave soon."

Mike groans and digs his head underneath his pillow.

"Time to get up. Don't make me call Chad."

Mike grumbles to himself and sits up, rubbing his eyes irritably. He stumbles blindly to the bathroom. The door slams and the shower goes on for a few seconds while Jeremy exchanges his tee for a light blue shirt. The shower shuts off, and the bathroom door opens at the same time as the dorm room door does.

Chad peeks in around the doorpost. Mike stands dripping in the bathroom doorway, blinking.

"Sorry," says Chad, entering and nodding courteously at Jeremy. "I should have knocked."

Jeremy shrugs and slings his tie around his neck.

Chad eyes Mike up and down. "Why did you take a shower with your clothes on?"

"Laundry."

"What are you talking about? I did your laundry for you yesterday. I hung it on your closet door."

Mike looks at Chad blankly.

"There," Chad snaps, gesturing towards the closet.

Mike shrugs.

"Thank you; that was so kind of you. You are the best brother I have ever had," Chad prompts.

"You're welcome," says Mike.

Jeremy muffles a laugh from his vantage point on his bed.

Chad turns and faces Jeremy. "I sincerely apologize for invading your privacy, Briggs."

"It's all good," says Jeremy. "But whatever you've gotta do, do it quick. Mike and I have to be somewhere."

"Oh, good. Mike needs to get out more often. Speaking of which," and here Chad turns to Mike, who is busy struggling into a fresh t-shirt from the laundry bag, "did you go to ANY classes today at all?"

Mike frowns in indifference. "I was sleeping."

Chad sighs. He turns to leave, but then turns back.

"Mike?" he says. "You really ought to phone Mother. She's worried about you."

"I never phone," says Mike, confused.

"Exactly. You should. Good day, Mike, good day, Jeremy." With that, Chad is gone, clicking the door shut firmly behind him.

Mike bends down to tie his shoes. "I don't want to go to a dumb party," he mutters.

"I know. I'm taking you to see the rabbi. No party."

"Rabbi?"

"Rabbi — like I told you last night. Rabbi Norton. He's a good guy. You'll like him."

Mike stares at something beyond Jeremy. His eyebrows rise, and his mouth purses. "Huh," he says. "A rabbi." A pause. "I'm not wearing a tie," he says and looks at Jeremy, his brow furrowed threateningly.

"Naaw, no ties. I just like to dress up when I see him. I feel like I should, because he's all holy. Don't worry about it."

"Hmm," says Mike, and he reaches for the car keys on 'Coffee Table'.

"You mean you're coming?"

Mike stuffs his keys into his jeans pocket and shuffles towards the door. "My car," he says.

Jeremy wonders with mild concern where Mike procured a car from. But still, "No car," he says. "It's just ten minutes. We'll walk."

Mike heads back to his bed.

"Fine," says Jeremy, "your car."

As always, he will regret this decision.

■ ■ ■

Tzvi hops back and forth from couch to armchair, his face glowing with excitement at the many guests who fill his home.

Rabbi Norton stands in a corner and speaks pleasantly to an art student with a goatee.

In the kitchen, Minna Norton removes a tray of piping-hot, chocolate nut cookies from the oven.

"Excuse me for a moment, Vergil," says Rabbi Norton. He enters the kitchen.

"Minna, did Jeremy call you?" he asks, helping himself to a cookie. "I thought he was coming."

"Oh, he is coming. He called me this morning and said he was bringing a friend of his, his roommate I think it was."

"Ah, so Mike is Jewish?"

"Seems so."

"Hmm. Jeremy's doing *kiruv* work already? That boy is really something special." He reaches for another cookie as Mrs. Norton whisks the tray away to safer grounds.

The students in the living room chatter and joke with one another. Yanky slips his way downstairs and into their midst.

Al looks down at the pudgy toddler, who smiles angelically up at him.

"Hey there, kiddo," says Al, and he scoops him up, awkwardly handling Yanky by wrapping an arm around him and squeezing his stomach.

"What are you doin'?" Philip yells, snatching Yanky away from Al. "That's not how to hold a kid. You gotta hold them gentle, like this. They can't hold their heads up by themselves, you know," and he cradles Yanky in his arms. Yanky grunts in protest.

"Look at him," says Mark. "You're going to make him cry. Give him to me." Yanky starts to fuss. "See?" He grabs Yanky from Philip, gripping his waist between two meaty hands. Yanky lets out a wail.

"You're such a bully. You made the kid cry," says Philip, a scowl of anger pressing his chin.

"I'll take him," says Tzvi, popping up at Mark's side.

"You're too little to hold him. You'll drop him," says Philip.

"No, I won't. I ALWAYS hold him."

"Um, guys, I think he needs to be, y'know, changed," gripes Mark.

"Aaw, man. Just put him down," says Al.

Minna comes to rescue Yanky just in time.

"Hey, Rabbi Norton," says Al, "when are we going to do this thing?"

"Soon," says Rabbi Norton. "We're just waiting for Jeremy and his roommate to show up."

"Jeremy Briggs?"

"Yes, that's the one."

"No way." Mark is suitably impressed.

"He was here last Shabbos," says the art student, shrugging.

"Dude...you speak to him?" asks Al.

"An ethereal experience, if I do say so myself. He really knows his stuff — we talked about light settings for almost fifteen minutes…"

"Is he, like, normal? You know, sometimes people like that are a little bit — "

"Hold the fort," says Philip. "He's bringing his roommate?!"

A stunned silence settles over the room.

Seemingly oblivious, Rabbi Norton nods pleasantly. "Yes, he's mentioned him before. I think his name is Mike — "

"He's Jewish?" says Al.

"He's coming?" says Philip.

"Don't interrupt the rabbi," hisses Mark.

Quite suddenly, from the distance come the sounds of startled honking and the squealing of tires around sharp bends at breakneck speeds. Philip peeks out of the curtains just in time to see a car coming down the wrong side of the street at 150 km/h. The driver slams down on the brakes two houses away from them. The car skids and begins to spin towards Rabbi Norton's house, and then slips neatly into the driveway, leaving burnt rubber in its wake.

"They're here," says Philip. "Mike drove."

Rabbi Norton tugs at the ends of his beard.

The door bangs opens and Jeremy enters, holding his arms out as if to embrace all the occupants of the room. "Let's get this party started," he says, grinning hugely around him.

Mrs. Norton peeks out from the kitchen. "Hello, Jeremy, good to see you again."

"Same here. So, well, we're here. Yeah, kind of late...thanks for waiting."

Rabbi Norton smiles and nods at him.

"Hi, Jeremy," says Mark, beaming at him, his face flushed in excitement. "My name's Mark. It's really good to see you. Um, I mean, not because I've never seen you. Of course I've seen you, heh...What I mean is...Okay, I'm shutting up." He looks to the side in embarrassment.

"Don't worry about it; good to see ya, too," says Jeremy, doffing him lightly at the side of his head. He steps past Mark, tugging Mike along with him. "Rabbi, I'd like you to meet Mike," and with a powerful shove, he sends Mike hurtling into Rabbi Norton.

Mike looks up at Rabbi Norton through a sheet of tousled hair.

"Hello," says Rabbi Norton, a warm smile crinkling around his eyes. "Welcome. I'm Rabbi Norton."

Mike jams his fists into his pockets and shuffles backwards, burrowing himself down into his hoodie. Rabbi Norton doesn't push it.

"All right, gentlemen, now that we're all here, let's gather around the table."

As they settle into their chairs, Philip is already holding up a finger for a question.

"Alright, Philip. One moment; I'm just going to explain how this works. First of all, any questions you have, please, go ahead and ask. But sometimes it happens that I may not be able to answer your question in the short time we have, which doesn't mean I'm ignoring your question or taking it lightly. I'm more than ready to answer you at a later time — after the session, or call me... *Nu*, ask. Always ask." And he smiles at all of them.

"Okay, can I go?" asks Philip, and Rabbi Norton nods at him to go ahead. "Right, so what I don't get, like, it's really bugging me? So...I get the whole thing about how obviously if G-d created us, we serve Him and all. But really, what difference does it make HOW, y'know? Like, as long as we recognize that He created us, isn't that enough? Just, kind of respect Him in our own way. And especially if we do it in the way we would serve the person we honor most — wouldn't that almost be better? Like, how can all this be one size fits all? Everyone has their own ways of honoring someone that works for them. You get what I'm saying?"

"Certainly. I understand. So I'm going to give you two ways to look at it. They both boil down to the same answer, but you choose what works best for you, okay?"

"I got it."

"First way to see it is very straightforward. Do you all know what e-mail is?"

Al chuckles. He wonders if Rabbi Norton means to be funny, but that won't get in the way of his amusement.

"And if you have not, we all, I should hope, have heard of the wonderful invention of the telephone. Now, what happens if, when you type in that address, you decide, 'I don't like how that dot looks there. I think I'll change it to a....a dash.' Or, how about you decide, 'It's easier to type in an entire phone number if all the numbers are the same digit.' But if you do that, it's not that it might not work just as well. It won't work at all! That e-mail will never be sent to the person you wanted it to go to. That phone call is going to end up contacting some Chinese person whose entire understanding of the English language is the word 'McDonald's.' In other words, deciding to serve Hashem in the way you see fit instead of the way it is commanded may be wonderful for you, but it's just not going to work.

"Now let me answer you with a different analogy. There's a famous inventor who comes out with this amazing machine and he invites you over to try it out. He tells you, 'Press that red button. And whatever you do, don't press the green.' Now, although you may have found that often, red buttons are not the sort of things you press, you would never argue with your friend and tell him that the green would be a far better choice. Why is this? Quite simply, because, seeing as he made the machine, he knows how it runs — not you."

The boys nod understandingly.

Rabbi Norton holds up his hands in surrender. "Seeing as you are MBU students, you are miles ahead with my thought process and you know what I'm about to say, but amuse me and let me finish up. I find it's best I articulate it.

"Every morning I say a special *tefillah*, a prayer, called *Ani Ma'amin*, where I state that I believe Hashem created the world. And if He created the world and He created us, then naturally one must conclude that He knows precisely what is best for us, and that yes, certain things in life are supposed to be followed by everyone."

"Wait. Hold it," says Al. "What's that supposed to mean? G-d wants us all to be the same?"

"On the contrary. If He wanted us all to be the same, He would have just made us like that in the first place. In fact, in Judaism there are all sorts of levels of hierarchy. There are the *kohanim*, the priests. There are kings, there are judges, etc., and everyone serves Hashem with their own unique capabilities. The Torah is not something which stifles the self in order to make us all one and the same. Rather, by having guidelines and rules, we are able to walk through life with more ease... Let me just think for a moment for the best way to explain....explain to you what Torah is.

"The Torah... The Torah is like a map. If you need to cross the desert, are you going to say to someone who offers you a map, 'Bah, who needs a map? It's so restrictive! I want to be myself. I am an individual. I can figure out my own way to do this!'? Obviously, you would take the map and follow it so carefully, it will be as if your nose is attached to the paper. You want to make it through the desert to your destination in the safest and easiest way possible! So, too, we must follow the Torah so carefully, so that we can cross through life and not wander around aimlessly."

"A map?" comes a voice, hesitant and quiet, and Rabbi Norton realizes with a start that it is the first time he has heard Mike speak.

"That's right. Do you have a question?" he asks Mike kindly, but Mike is silent once more.

"All right then. Who else? Ah! Jeremy, we haven't heard from you yet tonight. What's your question?"

■ ■ ■

A companionable silence has fallen over the room. Vergil talks with animated verve to Jeremy, who nods encouragingly at him.

Jeremy cradles a sleeping Yanky in his lap. Rabbi Norton sees Mark, Philip, and Al out the front door.

"Come again, boys," he says, his eyes crinkling with love.

"Oh, we will, Rabbi," says Philip.

"Bye!" Mark calls over his shoulder, waving vigorously.

Rabbi Norton closes the door softly and makes his way back into the family room. A chuckle rumbles up from his chest as he surveys the scene.

"Mike," he says softly to the boy huddled in the corner. "Mike."

Mike looks up at the rabbi with his beard and gentle way of speaking and the kindly, patient twinkle in his eye. Mike cannot look anymore, but he cannot look away, either, and he takes in a shaky breath. There is a tugging behind his eyes, a lump beneath his tongue, and a slowness to his thoughts.

The rabbi drags a chair over to the slumped figure. He sits on the edge of his seat and leans down towards him. They sit like that for a time, the rabbi and Mike, staring into each other's eyes. Finally, Mike looks away. He hugs his knees close to himself and wobbles his jaws from side to side.

"Rabbi?" says Mike in a voice so quiet that Rabbi Norton must lean over further and strain his ears to hear it. Mike's voice is raspy, like bicycle wheels on a gravel pavement, and he coughs gently before continuing. "Rabbi. I don't.....Sorry, I mean...I'm so....Rabbi, you know things, don't you?" and Mike rubs his nose with his thumb and forefinger. Rabbi Norton hardly dares to move.

"Can... Rabbi, I just want to know if, I mean, I don't know. I don't know what I'm supposed to be doing or thinking or anything.

I don't really care anymore. But you don't think. You seem to just...know. Rabbi — there's really a G-d?"

The question hits Rabbi Norton in the pit of his stomach and wrenches upwards to his throat. Suddenly, he wants to cradle Mike in his arms like a new baby, to cuddle him and protect him, to wipe all the pain and pent-up emotion away from the fragile and broken boy before him. He wonders how it is that a boy so young could be so old. He peers deeply into Mike's eyes, and a stubborn yet happy conviction rises up and bursts through him as he says:

"Of course there is, Mike. Of course." And he smiles, because he can share such a wonderful feeling with someone.

Mike blinks and chews his bottom lip, and he hears it. He hears the power behind those words, and he knows Rabbi Norton has said those words with pure clarity and utmost certainty, and he knows what Rabbi Norton says is true. Something inside him breaks and crumbles into fluttery movements of auburn peace, and he blurts out, "How do you know?"

"How do I know? Mike...if that's what you're really asking, you know, I could tell you. I could. But that's not what you want to hear. Is it?"

"No. Not now."

Rabbi Norton waits.

"You're so sure about it, Rabbi, that's all. No one ever...I mean, not where I come from, at least...no one is like that. And yet, I know you're right. When people say, 'Do you believe in G-d?' somehow it makes it all silly, like, 'Do you believe in magic?' But you talk about a G-d, and there is no doubt whatsoever in your words that you know He's there. Like He's here the same way I'm here and you're here and we're all here.

"I've never heard someone speak of G-d the way you do. And I just can't help thinking that I've been stupid. I've always known the world couldn't be the way I was told, but still...G-d is such a hard thing. It's so hard. I don't believe in all that G-d-thing-flying-around concept. Your G-d is different, isn't He? Still, I don't know about Him... It's the only thing that makes sense, though....and....now I just confused myself more."

Rabbi Norton smiles. "No, I think you're starting to figure it out all by yourself. But let me just say that, sure, He 'makes sense,' as you put it, but Hashem is more than making sense. Hashem IS sense, and He is beyond sense. You understand that?"

Like snow slipping off a window, like fog clearing up above an ocean's bay, like tarnish slowly being polished, something falls behind Mike's eyes. "Yes, Rabbi," he says, "I think I do understand."

And he raises his chin and looks around himself like a blind man who has just been granted sight and is thrilled, yet unsure of what to do with it.

CHAPTER 11
RAINFALL

"Where do I come from?" he asks himself. "Who created me? What is my purpose in life?" The stifling heat wearies him, and he fears this to be the end. A moan of anguish rises up in his throat as he leans against the smooth black surface, wondering if he will slip away into death, never knowing the answers to his many questions. He struggles to hold on as beads of perspiration dot his forehead. "No," he gasps, "no. Not yet. Please." But his pleas seem to fall on deaf ears. "Is this my fate?" he entreats. "To be as though I have never been? Shall I then evaporate into nothingness?"

"Hey, Mike, check it out!" Jeremy pops his head around the monitor. "I'm a snowman."

Mike tosses the remote at Jeremy's snowman hat. It hits the carrot right on the tip and the hat goes spinning across the room. Mike continues calmly with his game.

"Hey! Wha —"

"Take him back outside; he'll die in this heat," Mike says, changing his character onscreen to shield-mode.

"He'll die in this heat? I'll die in this heat. Man." Jeremy flops onto his bed. "I wish they'd turn down the heater. It's either too cold in this place or too hot. Heh…enjoy. I'm getting out of here tomorrow."

Mike's head bobs up. He pauses the game and regards Jeremy curiously. "You're going back to Australia for two weeks? That's stupid."

"Naaw, I'm piecing a crew together for the video I'm shooting this summer. L.A — I'm going to L.A."

"Huh."

"Wanna come with?"

"No. I'm…I think I'm gonna go home."

"What? Why? What'll you do there?"

"I don't know. Visit."

"Okay. Cool." Jeremy nods, but inside he feels slightly disappointed. Of course he didn't want Mike moping around campus all winter break, but Mike hasn't been moping around a lot lately. He is almost a normal person these days, since he'd started hanging out with Rabbi Norton. Jeremy had been hoping for a fully Crazy Mike comeback sometime soon. Such as, say…winter break? Not that he'd be there to join in the fun, but school spirit definitely needed a boost on the after-hours life. It was way more boring this year than last.

Man, he can remember last year's winter break. Barely anyone stayed on campus — just Mike, Jeremy, and maybe thirty other boys in their dorm, rappelling down the sides of the building using tied-together bed sheets...motorcycling through the empty hallways...playing basketball in shorts and tank tops in the slashing, fiery-ice snow.

He remembers the day Mike stepped into his life. He'd slept by himself until then, his room the only place of solitude for him on campus, his refuge from the grinning faces and eager greetings. He had come early that year to settle in, just after he'd received that award for his film *Silver Moon*.

Every time he created something, he felt it, he lived it, and he had been the wildness of the *Silver Moon*. The dangerous movements of *Silver Moon* consumed him. An ever-pressing urge filled him to run. Run. Run. An endless beat of booming and the clattering of heeled boots, a chase in an alleyway. Run. Run. His head hurt and he couldn't stand the world around him, and that day he could have wept in relief as he entered his cocoon of peace, his room. He crept under the covers, the beat clattering and pounding in him. He wished it would stop. And then someone said, "Hi."

Throwing off his covers, he stood and looked around. He saw no one. "Now you've done it, Briggs," he told himself. "You've been teetering on the line between genius and crazy for too long, and you've slipped onto the wrong side." That's when Mike had dropped from his perch between the crowning on top of the door and ceiling.

"Wha—?" Jeremy said. "How—"

"The force of pressure and muscles of STEEL, baby," said Mike, his eyes sparkling. "Whoooh!!!!!!!!!! The expression on your face was priceless! Ahahahaha!" And he ran and flipped midair onto his bed, hanging his head upside down from the edge and grinning at him like a little puppy dog. "I'm Mike! I'm Mike! I'm in college — man, I'm in COLLEGE!! Bring on the PARTIES! YEAH!" And he tossed himself in one fluid motion across the room and onto Jeremy's bed. "THIS IS AWESOME!!!!!!!!!"

"Quiet! You are such a noisy person," snapped Jeremy. He strolled up to an overstuffed duffel bag leaning up against the closet door. He grabbed the handle and turned on Mike. "Now. What is this?"

"A duffel bag."

Jeremy groaned into his hand. "You're in the wrong room," he said.

"Nope. Room 428."

"Noooo. I can't deal with this right now." And Jeremy collapsed onto what was now Mike's bed. "I need a nap," he said and promptly fell asleep.

When he awoke, Mike was gone, but his duffel bag remained and a monitor had been set up in the middle of the room. Shouts came from outside, and Jeremy stumbled to the window in time to see Mike jumping around like a super-ball on the roof of someone's jeep as it circled the parking lot at 10 mph, a hound of sophomore punks running behind it, whooping like banshees and pumping their fists. Jeremy felt his laugh bubbling up inside of him for the first time in weeks, and he guffawed at the sheer insanity of it all. Quite suddenly, that stubborn, insistent beat was gone...

Now Jeremy smiles at the memory of it. "Mike, remember when you first came, last year?"

Mike leans against his bed and a hint of a smile tugs at the corners of his lips. "Man, I was such a kid then…"

"Still are."

"Yeah….Wait, what?"

Jeremy laughs. "No matter how hard you try, you'll never catch up to my age."

"Aw, who wants to be twenty-three anyway?"

"Who wants to be a kid?"

"I'm not a kid." Mike's brow furrows dangerously.

"One more year to go still, kiddo. Sorry."

"Careful or I'll work out some credits, and next thing you know I'll be years ahead of you. You'll still be trying to pass exams, and I'll have my own job. Yeah, might pop by campus every now and then to say hi…"

"You love this place…so quit talking. Sheesh, I forgot how annoying you are when you talk. Like a train running on sugar."

"Hmm." Mike turns back to his monitor.

"Wha—? Just kidding with you, Mike. C'mon, let's go check out what's happening at North Wall."

"You go. I hate North Wall."

"No, you don't. You love North Wall. North Wall is Crazy Mike's territory."

Mike sighs in aggravation and squeezes down on the controller pad, causing his game character to do a spin kick.

"Aaw, Mike, snap out of it."

"I'm going to sleep. Have fun in L.A." With that, Mike curls up on the floor and falls asleep.

■ ■ ■

Ten o'clock at night, Rabbi Norton pulls into his driveway in his station wagon and gets out, hoisting a box out of the passenger seat. As he heads up the porch stairs, something flickers in the shadows of the porch. Rabbi Norton stops short. Slowly, he lowers the box onto the stairs below. He faces the shadows and calls out, "Hello?"

Mike emerges hesitantly, eyes downcast.

"Ah, Mike! Shalom aleichem."

"A-Aleichem shalom, Rabbi Norton."

"Come inside! I was just about to make myself a cup of coffee."

"No. I mean, I'd rather not."

"Alright then." And Rabbi Norton settles himself down on a porch chair.

Mike sits down on the one next to him. He tugs anxiously at the strings of his hoodie.

"Well, Mike, it's the start of winter break now, isn't it? Are you doing anything special?"

"I'm going home."

"Ah. That's great. Recharge your batteries."

"I never really go home, you know?"

"Well…you will be now, though, won't you? Surely your parents will be thrilled."

"I do not know how to handle them."

"Your parents?"

"They are…difficult."

"Mike, can I be honest with you?"

"As opposed to…?"

Rabbi Norton smiles. "All parents want from their children is to see them succeed; that is really what gives them joy. Nothing makes me happier than watching my sons learning together Motza'ei Shabbos when they're home, sitting at the dining room table and delving into the Gemara… Or when I hear from my daughter's teacher how special she is. In Judaism, we call this *nachas*."

"See me succeed?"

"They want to see you as an appreciated, upstanding young gentleman. For you to carry on and go past them."

"True." Mike nods his head curtly.

"Didn't you tell me to be honest?"

"Heh." A hint of a smile flits across Mike's face.

"Did I answer your question?"

"I still do not know how to handle them. I am not this…upstanding young gentleman."

Rabbi Norton leans back in his chair and thinks for a moment. Not on how one should treat his parents, of course, but rather if Mike is ready to hear it. *If he's asking*, thinks Rabbi Norton, *he must be ready*. "Are you asking me for guidelines, Mike?"

"Rules. Yes. When I am playing games, there are rules — who

to shoot, where to go. In school, there are rules — you must give in assignments, you have to pass exams. If I am to do something, I should be told how to do it, or I will not be able to. So there has to be rules to life. I know there has to be. I'm right about that, aren't I? And you can tell me, so why don't you tell me?"

"*Mai'seh shehayah* — a man once came to Hillel and asked him to teach him all of Torah on one foot... Tell you what, Mike. I can't teach you everything now. But if I can answer your original question...?"

Mike nods. "Please."

"It's a concept," says Rabbi Norton. "Your parents, in a partnership with Hashem, have brought you into this world. They are credited with giving you your most valuable commodity — your life. Not only did they give you this, there were all those nights when your parents stayed up when you cried, and all the trouble that you've told me you were... They've fed you, clothed you, taken care of you. So it is natural then, and also a commandment — '*kabed es avicha vi'es imecha,*' to honor your father and mother." Rabbi Norton beams, reveling in the beauty of this *mitzvah*. He looks over at Mike to gauge his reaction. Mike looks back expectantly, but Rabbi Norton rests his arms comfortably about his middle and closes his eyes in satisfaction.

Mike fidgets for time, waiting. Then he looks up at Rabbi Norton and asks, "But...but Rabbi Norton, what about the rules?"

■ ■ ■

It's eight a.m. when Chad clatters into the house, face beaming.

Claire has just sat to down to a cup of espresso and Ben's newspaper.

"Mother," he says, bending down and pecking her on the forehead, "it's good to be home."

"It's wonderful to see you, Chad," she says, folding the newspaper neatly and placing her mug on top of it. "Come, sit down next to me."

Chad pulls out a chair and sits down, shoulders back.

"Tell me what the professor told you."

"Well, he says that since I didn't fail the exam, he'll keep me in class. But he would like to see an improvement. I understand this, certainly. I shall be sure to apply myself more fully this coming term."

"Chad, honey?"

"Yes?"

"Are you sure you want to do this? Maybe another school would be more... suitable? We could transfer your credits. I am sure most schools would be thrilled to have a boy like you."

"But MBU is THE school, Mother! I must graduate there. I will. Or don't you think I can?"

"I just don't want you trying something that will make you feel dispirited."

"How so?"

"Your brother is —"

"Please don't compare me to him, Mother."

"I'm not comparing the two of you. I'm worried that you are, though."

"Why would I do that? No. No! MBU is about me. But speaking of Mike, where is he?"

"Mike?" Claire lifts a styled eyebrow. "He doesn't come home when he's in school, Chad. It's wonderful that you have. It's lovely to talk to you face to face. And about school...you know, Chad, that whatever you decide, you have my full support. But do speak to your father beforehand."

"Speak to me about what?" asks Ben, walking up to the espresso machine and finding it empty. He frowns at Claire's mug, then his eyes widen.

"My newspaper!"

"Oh, yes...that's right. It came on time this morning. I did mean to tell you."

Ben opens his mouth, then closes it. "I was ch-checking for it," he splutters, snatching it out from beneath the mug and stumbling off, rubbing his forehead in aggravation.

"Dear?" Claire calls after him. "Chad's come home."

"So I see," comes Ben's dry response from deep within the sports section.

Chad shrugs. "I thought Mike was coming. I was sure... At least, he gave that impression."

Claire gets up to rinse out her mug in the sink. "Mike doesn't come home, Chad, he just doesn't," she says, her mouth in a thin line as she turns the mug upside-down in the dish-drainer.

"Doesn't that bother you?"

"No, Chad. Mike just isn't that sort of boy, you know? He doesn't express himself or behave the way you do. And although you make me so happy with what a wonderful boy you are, I can understand that Mike is different. He got your father's, your uncle's, and my intelligence, but his personality is all his father's. It's a combination of the worst sort. People that smart...they often have a hard time expressing expected emotions. They can be self-absorbed and moody. They see the world in a different way than we do. Skipping him grade after grade only added to the problem...I'm beginning to think it was a mistake. Heaven knows I was aware of how much your father enjoys routine and stability... I think perhaps the reason why Mike doesn't visit, or call, or refer to us much when he's at school, is because he needs school and home to be separate. He doesn't want to mix these two parts of his world. It's easier for him to sort through life this way. You like to organize your life with file folders and paper clips. Mike organizes it all by rules and boundaries."

"That's...an interesting way of thinking."

"He's a genius, Chad. He'll never be the sort of son mothers expect. But I'm privileged to have such a son."

"Yes...a genius. Slightly insane is more like it."

"Oh, no, not at all. He's still so young, and...we made him see the focal point of everything as intelligence by always pushing him forward in that way... One of these days, he'll come around, though, now that he's finally found a school that he can't dance circles around. Meanwhile, Chad, you're the best thing that could have happened to him. Or me."

"Aaaw, Mother —"

"No, I've started telling you, and I'm going to finish this. I feel that it's very important."

Chad holds up his hands in surrender.

"I know how hard it is for you, having a younger brother grades ahead of you, proven to be smarter than you... But you've always handled it in the best way. You've been understanding, and you've become a person in your own right — a strong, charismatic, charming young man. A son any mother would be proud of. I started getting worried, when you insisted on going to MBU, that something was wrong. Chad, I never wanted you to feel that you had to be like your brother."

"But Mike is..." Chad's voice is thick.

"You are my pride and joy, Chad," says Claire, meeting his eyes and smiling. "Come, I took the day off. Let's go for a drive."

■ ■ ■

Time can be a very curious thing. It has a ways of eating itself up, leaving its victims stumbling after it, wondering where it went, knowing they can never pull it back.

Time always sneaks away from Mike, slipping through his fingers before he can grasp it tightly. He is loose, too loose, not caring, not holding on, and then time is gone.

He runs where his feet take him, past bake-shops and fire hydrants and billboards advertising Nike shoes. All he can see is a blur of slashing rain against his forehead, and all he can hear is the splashing water as it pours off rooftops. He is numb. He has been walking and running for hours, but he does not know it. All he knows is this pressing urge to move as his thoughts spin turbines around dizzy cycles in his head.

He was going to go in. He was. He'd prepared himself for the ordeal over and over again. He'd stood at the door of his home and stared at the solid oak doors. All he had to do was press the doorbell. Walk in. His fingers had stalled; his body rebelled. He couldn't do it. Didn't even know if he wanted to. Walking into his house, saying hello…it was like opening something he wasn't prepared to open yet. He had bolted.

Now he moves unconsciously through the city, released, panicked, weary and confused.

There had been a time, not so long ago, when such feelings were ordinary. The feeling of bubbled veins and wild laughter that could be controlled with speed and letting loose, but it seems that the harder he forces energy from himself, the more it fills him now.

Over and over he hears Jeremy's scream and the roaring in his ears from that time almost a year ago. The morning his view of the world shaded over.

■ ■ ■

"Man, that party was rockin'"

"Rollin'"

"Spinnin'"

"Bouncin'"

"Workin'"

"Awright, enough. I'm gonna have such a hangover tomorrow… my head is splitting already. Just get me to my bed, Mike."

"Uh-uh. You roll where I roll."

"Where's that?"

"The cliff line."

"Yeah, okay... we do need to calm it."

"Last time this year, Jeremy. All those evenings, tired, stressed, or whatever, we watched the sun come up over the cliff line. It always came up for us. And now we're going to say goodbye to the sun, and then next time we see it will be in the fall. I'll be seventeen, and you'll be one step closer to your dream of le famous director."

"You always gotta make things so dramatic, Mike?"

"Only when I'm drunk."

"You're not drunk. You're my designated driver."

"Heh. Right."

"...Don't tell your mom."

"Shut it. It was just a couple beers."

"You wouldn't be saying that if she was here."

"I said to shut it. Man, you're drunk."

"Thoroughly intoxicated," Jeremy said in an obnoxiously nasal voice.

"Who was that supposed to sound like?"

"What, you can't tell?"

"No."

"Aaaw, c'mon."

"No."

"It's so obvious. Just take a wild guess."

"Nope."

"Spoil sport."

"Yeah, I know." Mike pulled the speeding car into a sideways skid as he slammed on the brakes. "We're he-yere."

"Thank you for traveling The Bomb. Please remove all limbs and organs before exiting." Jeremy pushed his head against the seat back and unbuckled his seatbelt.

Mike somersaulted over the open side of the convertible.

"Hey, get back here and take your kidneys."

Mike shook his head and rolled his eyes, a grin lighting his face. "Those are yours, old man!" he called over his shoulder.

"You just wait...this old man isn't going to be taking that lying down."

Mike cackled, speeding up towards the cliff line. Jeremy bounded after him and they settled themselves side by side, feet hanging over the edge of the chasm.

As the sun peeked its head cautiously over the horizon, Jeremy felt Mike stiffen at his side. A burst of color spread over the midnight blue, and a globe of amber gold rose slowly on its voyage, sailing upwards to meet them, spilling its warmth over the rocks, and somewhere nearby a bird sang it a song of welcome. With a crackle of flaming orange, it finally climbed above the cliff, so it seemed to face them in expectation, seemed to level its warmth to fill them.

"Man..." gasped Jeremy, rubbing the back of his neck in utter amazement. "That wasn't...I never get used to it... It's like there's G-d painting it and all, while we watch."

Mike pulled his knees up towards his chest and glared forward. "It's just a sunrise," he said.

Jeremy felt like someone had tossed a bucket of cold water over his warm dreams. "Wha — hold it. Hey, you were the one who was always into it in the first place."

Mike shook his head irritably, and it seemed as though the fire of the sun had entered his veins, and he turned to Jeremy, gripping his arm. "It's just a sunrise."

He stood and looked about himself wildly. His chest heaved, and panicked craze seemed to rock his eyes. He ran off towards the car, turning back at Jeremy only to scream, "It doesn't mean anything! It's just a sunrise!"

"Alright," muttered Jeremy. "I get it. It's just a sunrise."

Mike jumped into the driver's seat and turned the key, revving the engine, the tires spinning up a cloud of dust into the morning air. He turned the car straight towards the cliff, slamming on the gas.

"Mike!" screamed Jeremy, but Mike threw himself out just as the car sailed over the edge and plummeted down the cliff face, turning horribly in a spiraling corkscrew and exploding in a dome of heat at the bottom.

"Whoo-whoo!" whooped Mike, pumping his fist in the air and jumping up and down. "Did you see that?! Huh? That was awesome! That was amazing. WHOOOOOO!!!" His voice echoed into the silence that followed the explosion.

Jeremy's face turned an unhealthy shade of purple. "What the... what the...why did you DO that, Mike?! YOU IDIOT!"

Mike shrugged. "I felt like it."

"No. Talk to me. What was that all about?"

"Nothing." *Mike seemed tired, the life slipping from his shoulders as he turned towards Jeremy. He shoved Jeremy in the general direction of the road.* "I just felt like doing it. Forget about it. Let's get back to school."

He walked off without bothering to check whether or not Jeremy was following, head down, hands jammed firmly into his pants pockets.

■ ■ ■

It's late, maybe eleven o'clock, maybe midnight. Claire usually keeps better track of time, but Chad has proven to be a wonderful distraction. She hadn't realized how much she enjoyed their evening discussions until he'd left for school.

The telephone just isn't the same as sitting across from a warm person, meeting his eyes, and sharing ideas and thoughts. No, the receiver is a cold, cruel replacement, and Claire and Chad have been talking as though they'd never spoken to each other before.

The timid rapping at the door goes unnoticed, but when the doorbell goes off for the third time in succession, Claire reluctantly gets up.

She throws the door open to the cold and wet outdoors. The porch light blinks on, and Mike stands there, his hands behind his back, shoulders slumped. Rivulets of rain run down his face, and his sweatshirt is stretched out by the weight of the absorbed water. He looks up through the screen of soaking hair plastering his face, his eyes turned upwards, facing hers, in nervous expectation.

"Mike?!" Claire says, covering her mouth with a manicured hand. She grabs the front of his sweatshirt and yanks him into the foyer. "Chad, towel!" Chad takes off in a gallop towards the washroom.

Mike steps back from her. "I'm getting the floor —"

"The floor can take care of itself very nicely. Mike, where is your coat?"

Mike removes his hand from behind his back and stretches it out towards Claire. "Here," he says, not meeting her eyes.

He holds out a bouquet of drenched daffodils, drops of rain sliding down its plastic wrapping. A card bleeds blue ink, reading: 'To a wonderful mom.'

"Why...these are beautiful, Mike," says Claire, her mind floundering and attempting to grasp these changing events.

Chad tosses a towel over Mike's head and proceeds to scrub vigorously at his brother's hair. "Mother is allergic to daffodils," he says. "They make her sneeze."

"No," protests Claire, trying to blink back tears, "I love them."

Mike reaches up a hand to stop Chad's. "Thank you, Chad," he says. "I think I'll go change now."

"Y-you're welcome," says Chad.

Mike shuffles off to his bedroom.

"Okay... That...was slightly disconcerting. What's with him?" asks Chad.

Claire looks down at the bunch of flowers, biting at her knuckles. "I suppose you were right, Chad. He *was* coming home."

■ ■ ■

"Mr. Briggs, your phone rang while you were out."

"Wha — oh, okay, one second." He turns to dump the stack of files he's been lugging into the arms of the person next to him. "Do something with these, Sandlers, will you? I gotta take the phone."

He tucks the phone between his ear and shoulder. "Yeah?" he says, distractedly.

"Jemmy?"

At the sound of her voice, he stiffens. He holds up a finger at someone who has been trying to get his attention, then turns on his heel and hurries out of the room.

He leans against the banister in the stairwell, holding the phone loosely between his fingers, gazing dispiritedly at a spider crawling up the length of the wall.

"Hello, Mum," he says. "What a surprise. How are you?"

"You know very well how I am, Jeremy. Now tell me, are you coming home? I've been waiting all week."

"No, sorry. I'm in L.A. working on a project."

"Working on a project? Too busy, I suppose, to visit your dying mother?"

"I'm sorry. I couldn't get away. I have a lot on my plate right now.

I'm trying to…put some things together. Sort stuff out."

"For all you know, you'll never see me again. What's more important to you, me or your silly —"

"Mum, the doctor says you're fine."

"Do not interrupt me, young man. And for your information, doctors don't know everything. I know I'm sick. I just know it."

"I'm an adult now, Mum, please try to understand. I have a life and an important job. I'm practically famous now… You've got a famous son. Doesn't that make you happy?"

"Oh," she wails, "Jeremy, please, why are you leaving me all alone? You haven't been home in four years. Come visit."

"I just came home last summer."

"For two days. TWO DAYS. You don't care about me at all. All you care about is —"

"That's not true."

"Oh, yes, it is. Otherwise, it wouldn't hurt you the way I know it does. You feel guilty now, don't you? I know my own son."

"Did you go and see my latest production in the theater? *A New Ending*?"

"Of course not. It was raining."

"Every night? For two months?!"

"Don't scream at me," she bawls and sniffles.

"Don't cry. Come, Mum. Please…don't cry."

"Oh, yes, I will. No one ever thinks about me in this family. Your good-for-nothing sister left me all alone to take care of you when you were just a baby. I had no help whatsoever. She just up and married that horrible Morris. And your father…all that man cares about is his rotten work. He's always in the office. He never comes home. He won't talk to me; he hardly notices me. I don't know why… I never should have married that man. I knew it. I knew it was a mistake to marry him from the moment I walked down that aisle. And now you. You've left me, too."

"I didn't leave you, Mum. I'm still here; you talk to me plenty on the phone. I'm just really busy these days, what with school and my projects and…life in general. Please try to understand."

"Why? Why? Come home, Jemmy. Mummy's going to take care of you." She bawls horrendously over the line.

Jeremy slumps down onto the cold tile stairs. "Look, Mum…I have to go. I'm sorry."

"Don't you dare hang up on your own mother!"

"Love you," says Jeremy and cuts off the call.

He rests his forehead on his knees for a moment, staring at his sandaled feet. Then he shudders slightly and in a fit, hurls his cell phone down the stairs. It sails across the landing below and smacks against the wall, clattering to the ground in a buzz of electricity as shock protection sets in.

■ ■ ■

Ben knocks on Gordon's door on his way out.

"I'm leaving, Gordon," he says. "Need a lift?"

"No. Thanks. I need to finish…" He waves his hand at a stack of papers.

"I could probably find something to do meanwhile."

"It's going to take a while — a real mess here. Don't wait for me."

"Okay. Good evening."

"Good evening."

"Oh, Gordon?"

"Yep?"

"Did you happen to take a look at MaxCom's figures?"

"No. Why?"

"They've almost dropped out the bottom."

"What?! How's that?"

"Their products are messed up...it's too complicated. Tell you tomorrow."

"No, now."

"No, tomorrow. Good evening, Gordon."

Once again Gordon finds himself glaring at a neatly shut door.

■ ■ ■

Traffic is surprisingly light coming home; Ben arrives ahead of schedule. He punches his fingerprints in at the side door.

"I'm home!" he calls to no one in particular. He is halfway to the kitchen before he remembers that Claire had called him at the office to tell him she'd be home late with Mike. That means supper is far from ready.

Ben frowns. Hunching his shoulders, he continues on to the

kitchen. There he finds Chad, sitting at the breakfast table, busily scribbling away in a notebook, calculator handy.

Chad looks up as Ben approaches the table. "Oh, good evening, Dad. How was work?" he says.

"Okay, as far as days go. What about you? How did your boss take your leaving?"

"Oh, he's okay with it. He was a bit upset about having to find a stand-in on such short notice, but my schoolwork has to take precedence. I was just drowning in all that work."

"Hmm...stand-in?"

"Oh, yes, of course. You didn't think Mr. Ryerson would have me replaced, would you?"

"Well...seeing as you've got quite a few years of school to go, I wouldn't have expected him to wait around. But congratulations, son. Seems like you'll have a job waiting for you when you're done with everything."

"Yes. I figured that's important. Busy hands stay out of trouble, wouldn't you agree, Dad?"

Ben regards his son, his jaw slanted. "That's the spirit," he says, although he is quite sure it isn't. He finds it difficult to relate to this son. At times he wonders how such a child could have come about through him. "Anything to eat?"

"I saw some bologna in the fridge before."

"Hey, look at that. My son knows what I like." Ben eases out of his jacket and hangs it on the back of a chair before rummaging in the fridge. "Where does she keep it?"

"Meat bin."

"Meat bin...what's that?"

"Um....below the third shelf."

"The glass one?"

"No, it's white —"

"Could you come here and show me?"

"Dad! I am exceedingly busy at this present moment in time."

"But I don't — oh, here we are. Aaaaaaaaaaah, nothing like a good sandwich. Okay, pickles...cheese...ketchup...mustard...mustard, mustard, mustard — oh, there it is. What else do I need...? Bread! Imagine trying to make a sandwich without — oooh FEGARO DaDaDaDEE, DEE DOH DEEDAY, DA DO LALAAA —"

"Dad!"

"Okay, okay, I'll be quiet."

Ben slaps the top slice down on his three-inch-thick sandwich. He takes it to the table and settles himself comfortably in his chair. He lets out a sigh of contentment as he chews his way through his monstrosity.

"Hey, Chad," he says, using his forefinger to wipe off some dribbled mustard from his tie, "have you been keeping up with the Maple Leafs this season?"

"Yes, Dad, of course, Dad."

"Well, did you see last night when that guy got slam-checked WHAM into the glass? Blood everywhere! They had medical people in there and everything. Went right back to the game afterwards, of course. The one who did it got away with it completely. Think that's fair?"

"Dad, I'm sorry, I didn't catch that part. As you can see, I've been pretty busy lately."

"Oh. But still, in general. What do you think of all this dirty playing? They never did that sort of thing when I was your age. Of course, as I remember, they didn't wear helmets either... How about we go watch the game together sometime? Tonight I'm free — I can get us tickets. What do you say?"

"There's nothing I'd enjoy more. However, if I don't manage to finish my work —"

"Super! I tell you, there's nothing quite like the game. It's what brings people together. The spirit...nothing like hockey. I love it. Mike and I used to play the game on his...watchamacallit...that you play games on...? We don't anymore, of course. But still, it was never the real thing — I get an adrenaline rush just being in those stands."

"Great. That's wonderful."

"Did you —"

"I have to make a phone call."

Chad shoves his chair away from the table and stands, unclipping his cell phone from his belt loop. He turns and exits the kitchen, dress shoes clicking down the hall towards the library.

Ben licks his finger and dabs the table surface with it, collecting the last vestiges of crumbs. He sucks on his finger as his mind puzzles over his son.

Whatever happened to childhood? Kids these days — they're either far too immature or too mature, no nice, steady balance. The same way, it suddenly hits him, the very same way it is with everything. Anorexia or obesity. Big boss or little loser... And why in heaven's name does his son want to work so hard, anyway? Mike never works at all. Probably relying on inheritance to tide him through life. Won't the fellow be disappointed to find that he, Ben, is going to live for a very long, long time.

Frankly, Ben can't wait to be a grumpy old man, making rude remarks, instructing his daughters-in-law in how they should be raising his grandkids, and forcing passerby to listen to long-winded stories of his youth and growing up in Manitoba.

Absently, Ben reaches for Chad's notebook and flips slowly through the pages. As he does so, his brow grows more and more furrowed, and the clouded sense of calm seeps from his eyes, and his jaw rests firmer and firmer against his neck.

Chad returns a few minutes later to find his father gone. His notebook is not where he left it.

"Dad?" he calls, and still louder, "Dad?!"

He slips his notebook under his arm and twists himself around. In hurried bounds, he takes the stairs. He bursts into his room. His eyes roll furiously to take in the scene. His father is sitting on his bed, a pile of notebooks stacked at his side, flipping frantically through them, one by one.

"Dad?"

Ben looks up at Chad and fixes him with a stare that sends shivers up and down Chad's back.

"This is not what it looks like, Dad. I can explain."

"There's nothing to explain. It's pretty straightforward. Meticulously recorded. A fool could understand it."

"No, this is not what it looks like, really, it's not."

Ben stands up and throws the last notebook down on the bed with a smack. He does not look at Chad. He marches out of the room. Chad follows him.

"Rob told me to do it. I was doing him a favor."

"Oh, I'll bet."

"He did, Dad, honestly. No, why would I do it otherwise?"

"I don't know, Chad. Why would you stab your own father in the back?"

"You see? Exactly."

Ben pauses at the top of the stairs. Chad hurries to catch up.

Ben grips the handrail, his knuckles white. "I don't think so, Chad. I think that's a whole lot of garbage you're telling me."

"But I —"

"Rob might be slightly unorthodox, maybe even a bit crazy, but he isn't stupid. I can't believe something like that. And look at all you managed to do! Where did you even find the time for it all?"

"Dad —"

"I don't want to hear it."

"I'm feeding them false information. That's the whole job, okay?"

"Chad..."

"No. Dad, listen to me. I promise! I was —"

"I know exactly what you were doing! I...Chad, I can't even look at you. I can't...it's disgusting! I mean, HOW COULD YOU?! Do you have absolutely no respect left for me at all?!" Ben paces the length of the stairwell like a caged bear, his face red and sweating.

"I do, I really do, Dad. I look up to you tremendously. That's why I was trying to help —"

"Ha! Some help!"

"What's going on?" asks Claire, who has just entered through the side. She kicks her high heels off on the mat at the front door and heads up the stairs towards them. "What are you two getting so worked up about?"

"Stay out of this, Claire!" howls Ben, holding his palm outward at the side of his head like a crossing guard.

"I will not. Are you boys fighting?"

"We. Are not. FIGHTING!"

"Please don't raise your voice to me."

"I AM NOT RAISING MY VOICE!"

"Dad, just talk to Rob," Chad interjects. "He'll explain it to you."

"No," Ben says, looking down and to the side, "I'm not going to tell Rob yet. You're still my son. I...have to figure something out." His voice quivers.

"If I'm your son, then why don't you believe me?"

"Because I'm not an idiot!" Ben turns and storms down the stairs.

"But it's the truth!"

Ben's shoulders slump. "Quiet!" he roars. He shakes his head in irritation and walks slowly to his study. "I need time to think," he says, and the door swings shut behind him.

"Oh, dear," whispers Claire, and she hurries off to the kitchen to make Ben's favorite dinner.

Chad collapses onto the last step and hides his face in his hands.

From the hallway off the side door, two eyes peek through a curtain of wild hair. Mike grips the doorpost and something flutters inside him, banging at the edges of his stomach. Panic rises slowly upwards, threatening to strangle him, as his mind works desperately to understand. What is happening to his family? This is not how it's supposed to be. Why are they fighting? They never fight. Why is everything changing?

Don't change.

Please don't change.

■ ■ ■

"Bye, sweetie!" Claire smiles, her arms folded tightly around her waist. "Take care!"

"Goodbye, Mother. I'll call you the moment I arrive." Chad looks over at Ben. His mouth opens as if to say something, but clamps shut as Ben turns around and faces the stair landing.

"Mike! Coming?" Ben calls up the stairs.

"One sec..." Mike shuts the door of his room behind him and slings a canvas rucksack higher up on his back. He comes downstairs slowly, watching his feet's movements and nothing but. Finally he reaches Ben and looks up at him.

"See you, Dad." A small smile lights up his face. "It's been fun."

"Yes, it has. You take care, son."

They nod at each other.

"Cleaned my room," he says to Claire, hopping from one foot to another anxiously. "Um…bye, Mom."

She smiles at him, eyes widened in nervous expectation. "Mike, Chad's driving. I know it's your car, but, just…let me feel safe, okay?"

Mike's jaw tightens, but he nods bravely.

Claire and Ben watch from the doorway as Chad pulls out of the four-car garage and reverses backwards out the circular driveway. As the car circles around the corner and out of sight, Claire sighs. Ben shrugs his shoulders back and closes the front door.

"I'm gonna make us both some good, strong coffee," he says and hurries off towards the kitchen.

Claire follows. She sits down at the edge of a kitchen chair as Ben adds the ingredients to the coffee machine.

"Well, now…" she says, "that has been quite an experience."

"I'll say," says Ben, choking back a hysterical bark of laughter. "I mean, I never thought that Chad —"

"Oh, forget about Chad for a moment, will you?"

"Forget? Forget?!"

"It was just a silly little bit of nonsense. Ben, we've gone through this one too many times this week. Right now we have to discuss Mike."

Ben sighs and leans his back against the counter, facing Claire.

"What about Mike?"

"I don't know. You might think I'm being slightly paranoid, but… that wasn't the Mike I saw off to school this fall."

"I guess not. He's almost himself again, isn't he? No, he's better!"

"Ben, he cleaned his room."

"He went to the hockey game with me."

"He agreed to go shopping with me. He let me buy him a suit."

"He got up seven every morning to buy me my newspaper."

"What are we going to do?!"

Ben looks up from his pleasurable wonder in sudden confusion. "Eh?"

"Do you not see the problem here?"

"Nope. Problem? I can't believe it… It's great!"

"No, Ben, it is not great."

"Why not?"

Claire sighs and puts her face in her hands. "I asked Chad if he knew what had…what had come over Mike. And he told me that there's this rabbi coming on campus and talking to Jewish boys. Inviting them to his house. Teaching them things."

"Okay. So? I once knew a rabbi. Nice enough fellow. As long as Mike's happy —"

"Are you not listening to me, Ben? Or don't you care? My son has been brainwashed by this, this, this man! What are we going to do about this?"

"Nothing. Claire, be reasonable."

"I am being reasonable. I am being perfectly reasonable! It's you who is not. My son is off being manipulated by some sort of cult, and all you want to discuss is Chad —"

"Yes, that is correct! Mike is fine. On the other hand, do you have any idea what Chad has done?! I don't even know what to —"

"Stop it, Ben. This is not about Chad! You just can't admit that there's something wrong with Mike. He's always been your favorite, hasn't he?! You've never liked Chad. Your own son. Now Chad made one mistake and instead of concentrating on —"

"For the last time, there is nothing wrong with Mike!"

"...He's still a minor, you know. I can sue."

"Claire, please. Don't you want what is best for him? If this is what Mike wants, why should we interfere? It's not as though there's any harm being done. Let's not overreact —"

"This discussion is over!" shrills Claire. "Now, are you going to call that lawyer, or am I?"

CHAPTER 12
THE PLOT THICKENS

"...And Briggs heads across the court at 200 miles per hour...And he aims!...And he fires!...And he SCORES! Awright!" Jeremy pumps his fist into the air. "I am the king, I am the master, I am ultra-OWW!" The basketball hits him in the side of his face. "Watch it, you!"

He chases after Al, who runs across the court in the opposite direction, plowing through the others head-first with the basketball tucked securely in the crook of his arm. Phil tackles him. They tumble to the concrete in a blur of legs and arms. Jeremy dives on top of them, howling, "GERONIMO!"

The ball slips to the side and rolls to Mike's feet, where he hunches at the wall of the shul. He picks it up and stands, throwing it half-heartedly at the net. It swooshes through neatly.

"Nice," says Vergil, who is sitting on the grass by the fence and keeping score.

"Hey! The silent one has joined!" says Phil. "You're on mine and Al's team!"

"It's too cold for basketball," says Mike, heading into the shul.

"Wha — HEY! Fine, whatever. It would have been uneven then, anyway." Al kicks at the ball, pop-flying it onto the roof.

"Nice," says Vergil, humming, feeling nature down to his core as Al's glare sails over his consciousness.

Phil groans in frustration. "Now what?"

"Mark, you can climb, right?" says Jeremy.

Mark nods vigorously, his face lighting up.

"Here, I'll give you a boost. Step on my hands." Al stretches out his arms underneath the second floor window.

■ ■ ■

Inside the shul, Mike shuffles towards the kitchen, where he can hear the sounds of conversation and someone washing dishes. Rabbi Norton? He stops by the doorway because it's just Mrs. Norton washing some coffee mugs. There's someone with her, sitting at the kitchen table. He leans against the wall, trying to think where to go check next.

"So I'm gone. I'm totally just out of here."

"That must have been a hard decision to make."

"It really was. Like, seriously, I must have ordered and cancelled my ticket, like, seven times. I haven't slept in weeks. But I'm glad

I made it, you know? Like, now that I made up my mind, the pressure's off me and all. I can relax. It's a total relief."

"So you're really going this time?"

"Really! I'm SOOO serious. My bags are packed and everything. I'm signed up for a whole thing at this seminary, I'm gonna do the Kotel...everything!"

"Where are you staying when you first get there?"

"That rabbi's house from the first time I was there. He got me a small secretary job until the sem thing starts."

"Well, that's nice. I'm so proud of you, Shelly."

"Aaaaw...Rebbetzin...now I'm embarrassed."

"Don't be. You should be proud of yourself, too. Can I ask you how you decided?"

"It was kind of like a two-o'clock-in-the-morning type of thing. I just kind of said to myself, 'Shelly, stop it. Just make up your mind already. What do you want out of life?' I guess it wasn't as hard for me, though, because I already made a huge deal of it, what with my family and Greg, so it would have been hard to turn back anyway."

"It's never easy."

"K."

"Shelly, really. You have got to stop —"

"Aha! Mike!"

Mike bunches up into his sweater, peeping out with startled eyes. Rabbi Norton stands on the stairs leading up to the guest apartment, tie slightly askew, screwdriver held aloft.

"Good to see you! Shalom aleichem. I would shake your hand, but mine is filthy."

Mike nods. His head is spinning with what he just heard. What does he really want from life? he wonders. It's weird, like an ultimatum. Do some people need that? Shouldn't it be obvious?

"Who else is out there? I hear noises."

"People."

"People? I love people! Hold on one second while I put this away and let's go out and say hello to them." Rabbi Norton shoves the screwdriver into the hall closet, and he and Mike walk in sync outside.

"I found him," Mike announces as they exit the back door together.

"Hello, people!" says Rabbi Norton.

"Hey, hey, it's the rabbi!" says Jeremy, grinning and heading towards the Rabbi for a hug.

"Hey, Rabbi! Think fast!" Mark screams from the roof. The basketball comes hurtling downwards.

Al snatches it mid-air. "You trying to kill him?"

"Get me down from here," says Mark.

"Get yourself down."

"Here, I'll catch," says Jeremy, holding his arms out wide.

"Ha ha. I'll get down myself." Mark swings off the edge of the roof, catches his fall by latching onto the second-floor windowsill with his fingertips, and then lands like a cat on the courtyard. Rabbi Norton peeks through spread fingers in relief.

"Rabbi, you worried about me? I've been rock-climbing for years!" Mark pats Rabbi Norton on the back. "I can take care of myself."

"So I see," says Rabbi Norton.

"C'mon, Rabbi! Going to join us?"

"And how would one go about playing this game?"

Mike chuckles.

"Basketball?" says Phil in disbelief.

"Rabbi," says Al, smiling hugely, "you're the best! You are SO not cool!"

"*Baruch* Hashem," says Rabbi Norton.

■ ■ ■

The encyclopedia weighs comfortably down on the ends of Chad's fingers as he heads down the hall, whistling Beethoven's Ninth Symphony.

An elbow suddenly smacks into his side, stopping him abruptly. The encyclopedia clatters down onto his foot.

"How's it going," says Cole, nodding curtly at him.

"Very well, thank you," says Chad, rubbing his foot against the back of his leg, biting back a wince.

"Chad, right?"

"Yes, that's me. How can I help you?"

"I just wanted to mention how...brilliant your economics presentation was."

Chad's left eye twitches. "I didn't notice your presence there."

"A summary's coming out in the MBU magazine about it, right? It's gotta be good, I figure." He bears his teeth in a pathetic excuse for a smile.

Chad nods, smirking. "I worked on it with Mike. We work well together-"

"Oh, yeah! I heard a rumor that Mike's your brother." Cole's eyes glint.

"That would be correct." A frown creases Chad's brow.

"You two are both really, really intelligent individuals."

"Why, thank you," says Chad, glancing at his wristwatch.

"I guess you'd think I'm pretty dumb compared to you," says Cole, eyes gazing steadily at Chad's face for a reaction.

Chad's eyes snap up in stressed confusion. "I don't see why I would," he says. "Why do you ask?" He waits impatiently for the punch-line; he has other things to do today.

"Well," says Cole, triangulating his eyebrows in the perfect earnest expression, "thing is, I kind of got this reputation... You see," and he shrugs his shoulders, shoving his fists into his tattered jean pockets, chains clinking, "you see, I'm not like how people see me."

"No?" says Chad, unable to keep the sarcasm from seeping into his voice.

"No." Cole sighs and leans against the wall, looking up in practiced despair. "Truth is, I'm just a very sensitive, artsy type of guy, but...I kinda had a hard life...and, well, you know... But it's amazing how I'm able to just tell you this. I figure you don't judge me for it." He looks up at Chad with another toothy smile. "I hope we end up good friends."

"Uh-huh," says Chad, feeling vaguely disconcerted.

"Listen, I want to hang out with you more these days."

"Of course," says Chad, bending down to lift the encyclopedia and brushing past Cole in an attempt to appear in control of the situation.

Cole is up to something. Chad isn't stupid; the whole situation is very fishy.

And yet, what Cole had told him...it could be Cole just wants to be friends with someone normal for a change.

Maybe Cole is just being honest.

One never knew.

A quick shiver runs up Chad's spine and he squares his shoulders, pushing all disturbing thoughts away from his conscience. Taking a deep breath, he strides purposely away from the events and towards a hopeful day in the central library.

Back in the hallway, Cole snickers into his collar. Glee bubbles up inside him like soda, ending in barely suppressed guffaws. That had been just too easy. He'd learned it a long time ago: Some people are just too stupid for words.

■ ■ ■

The cell phone buzzes like a lawnmower, out of Jeremy's reach, on the computer monitor. Its vibrations cause it to spin in a circle before falling off the monitor and landing with a thud on the floor. The vibrations stop for a few seconds, then resume.

Jeremy groans and shoves himself out of his bed. He checks the caller ID, and a strange, humorless expression crosses his face. His thumb jabs down on the red button, and the phone screen lights up its shutting-off display. Then he calmly places the phone back on the monitor and proceeds to tear up a pad of paper one sheet at a time.

He is out of ideas for a new creation. Nothing is coming to him; there is nothing there. He's used up all his ideas, but he must think of a new one again. Something will come to him, just like something always comes to him.

Down under and in another hemisphere, Mrs. Briggs' nostrils flare dangerously. Her hand flutters nervously in the air. That rotten, no-good son of hers. He is avoiding her. She just knows it.

CHAPTER 13
RECKONINGS

Mike's back pops satisfactorily as he stretches himself out on the floor. "Done!" he announces, but when he looks over at Jeremy's bed, all he sees are the blankets thrown back and a wrinkled sheet. He checks the bedside clock and it reads 8:30. Morning? How could it be morning already? He hasn't gotten a chance to sleep yet.

He drags himself to the window and peeks out. He is surprised to see green grass and birds and a bright blue sky. What's today? Oh, yeah...it's sometime in May, isn't it? With a groan, he slumps down, banging the back of his head on the window ledge.

I need coffee, he thinks, rubbing his scalp distractedly. Then: *Where's Chad?*

He feels disoriented. His laptop beeps with yet another instant message from Miss Farren.

Things have been pretty busy lately, what with his project reaching completion and then trying to finish all those CLEPS, but he hopes that soon he'll be able to close this chapter of his life. Maybe he could. He would.

There is a polite rapping on his door and Chad enters with a Starbucks coffee. "Good morning," he says, breezing in and opening the window to let in some fresh air. "Been up all night, have we?"

Mike nods.

"Well, c'mon, up, up, up. Your physics professor asked me to tell you that the term paper is due soon."

Mike reaches lazily beneath his bed and scrabbles his hand around, coming out with some papers. "Physics..." he mutters. "Guess I can give him this."

Chad shrugs and takes the papers from Mike. "I don't know why they put up with you."

"Dunno why I put up with them."

"Fair enough. But I will say that I am confident you will get a beautiful mark, seeing as I cannot decipher a word of this. That's always a pretty clear indication..."

A small smile crosses over Mike's face and he looks up at Chad. "Number patterns of velocities."

"Oh, is that what those...squiggles..."

Mike lets out a hoarse and breathless laugh.

Chad sets the coffee down carefully on the edge of 'Coffee Table'. "Nice and cold, just as you like it."

"Thanks."

"It's just the usual that I always get you."

"Thank you."

"Okay... Well, have yourself a nice day, Michael."

He is close to leaving when Mike looks up suddenly. "They're just using you, you know," he says, yanking on his hoodie's strings.

"Who?"

"Them."

"I'm sorry, Michael, but I haven't the slightest idea what we are discussing right now."

"Cole. We're discussing Cole. Didn't you say that you had to concentrate on your studies this term?"

A dark cloud seems to descend on Chad's countenance as his nostrils flare and his chin wobbles. "I'll do as I please, and it's no concern of yours. What are you trying to do, rub it into my face that you don't need to study? Hmm?! Is that it? And since when did you become such a saint that you feel you can lecture me, you little, perfect little...perfect little...goody-two-shoes, daddy's boy, BRAT! Cole and me are tight, dig?" The word "dig" rolls painfully off Chad's tongue.

"I'm sorry. I just thought I'd..."

"Take your nose out of what I'm doing."

As Chad turns to leave in a self-righteous huff, he meets the hulking torso of Cole. "Ah, Cole! Good morning! And how are we today?"

"Outta my face," growls Cole, shoving Chad out the door and slamming it closed.

Mike gazes dispassionately at the carpet fibers in his slumped position below the window. It's Him.

Cole cracks his knuckles one at a time, then gives his hands a quick shake. "Where's Briggs?"

"Not here."

"Nooooooooooooooooooooooooooooo. You gotta be kidding me."

"Not at all. Perhaps you would like to have a look, though."

"Wanna shut it, kid?"

"Not really, no."

There is a long pause. Cole shifts legs and eyes Mike carefully. "So you the one been keeping Jeremy so busy these days?"

"Jeremy is busy on his own. He doesn't have time for you."

"Did I ask for your opinion?"

"If you didn't want it, why did you ask me that?"

Cole clenches his teeth and his unhealthy complexion turns an attractive shade of scarlet. "You know, everybody thinks you're so cool. They're all like 'Mike this' and 'Mike that'. But I don't think so. I think you're a loser."

"That's nice."

The ends of Cole's nostrils raise in a snarl. "You see Jeremy, you tell him I want his ugly face in my room pronto, you got me?"

"Nope."

"Watch it, you. One of these days..." Cole raises a brass-knuckled fist and shakes it threateningly, lips folded out of sight in a tight mouth. "One of these days...! You better be careful."

Mike glances through him in apparent boredom.

Cole squeezes up his biceps and his eyes shoot flaming sparks at the crumpled figure, maintaining self-control only because he dare not lose it on Mike Burns, child protégé and beloved campus mascot. Dumb kid.

"Stay out of my way!" he growls and exits the room in a consuming rage.

Mike notices with slight irritation that Cole left the door open.

■ ■ ■

"I don't know. I don't know if she's serious. I just don't know. I mean, probably not, right? She couldn't possibly mean it. But every once in a while, she'll threaten to call the lawyer... Claire is usually so level-headed and understanding, and all of a sudden it's as though... I mean, I personally think it's great. You know what Mike was like before he met the rabbi person — he wasn't even human. He was this cold machine walking around. Empty calculations and hollow antagonism and...and...all that sort of thing. And now...he respects me. He acts like a real son — calls me up once a week and talks to me on the phone. Just calls me up and talks. Tries to speak to Claire, too, but she doesn't seem to like it. She wants to sue that rabbi, but I don't get it. Well, she's your sister, so you tell me why she's like this." Ben clutches his armrest and looks at Rob in anxious perplexity.

"Oh, hidden passageway!" Rob advances his character past a sewer grate.

"Rob?"

"Hmm..."

"You listening?"

"Why can't I use my flash in this mission? That's not fair."

"Never mind. It was nice to get it all out there. But I wish you would at least pretend to care about other people." Ben gets out of his seat and onto the platform to descend to the floor below.

"I just got 5000 points. Ben, you gotta come here and look at this!"

"Good day, Rob."

The moment the carpet rolls back into place, Rob pauses his game and pulls out his new cream stationery. He clicks the back of his pen in and begins to write: *I hope all is well with you. However, I thought I should inform you that your dealings with my nephew are illegal...*

A button on his panel flickers. Rob clicks his tongue and the communicator blinks. "Sir — it's done."

"Great, Miss Farren. Then we better set it all moving... Um, listen, can you find me the address of a Rabbi Norton living near MBU?"

"No problem," says his secretary.

"Thank you. Oh, guess what?"

"What, sir?"

"I found a secret passageway!"

"Glad to hear it, sir."

■ ■ ■

Pencil shavings litter the floor like confetti below wadded up balls of lined paper. Jeremy sits on his bed, binder pressed into his lap as he scribbles vigorously. Quite suddenly, an alarm pierces the air and Mike's snoring comes to an abrupt halt.

Jeremy's train of thought is completely lost. His shoulders tighten in aggravation and he leans closer to his binder, scribbling up the margins of paper.

With a groan, Mike rolls out of bed and onto the floor, still tangled in his sheets. He yawns hugely and sits up, kicking some crumpled up paper out of his toes' way.

"You actually own an alarm clock?" asks Jeremy, pausing in his fruitless work to look at Mike with disbelief.

Mike moans and slams his head down onto his mattress. "I bought it so I could...get...up."

"What do you need to get up for?"

"Um..." says Mike as his sleep-deprived brain attempts to muddle out what the purpose of this particular torture is. He reaches for the cup of coffee Chad left for him on the monitor.

"It's eleven in the morning. Since when do you get up that early? And you went to bed when I got up."

"I was going to...I was going to...oh!" With that, Mike staggers to his feet and stumbles blindly in the general direction of the washroom. The door closes and Jeremy hears water splashing one-two, one-two, one-two. Then Mike re-emerges.

"Heh," says Jeremy, watching water droplets slip off the end of Mike nose and chin, "I remember when I had to worry about pimples."

"*Negel vasser.*"

"*Negel* who...? Oh right, that stuff. But speaking of which, I ever tell you about my dentist? His name's Nigle. Crazy guy, right? One time I come into his office with a throbbing — you got up early to study?"

Mike looks up from the small leather book on which he's been concentrating. "No...to pray, um, *daven*. I finished learning how to read the Hebrew alphabet online last week...now I can do this."

"Okay, cool. No, wait. You gotta say that whole book?!"

"I...I hope not. Maybe I should call the rabbi." Mike tucks the siddur into his hoodie pocket, softly and with care. He picks up his cell phone from 'Coffee Table', dialing Rabbi Norton's number with his left thumb.

Jeremy scratches behind his left ear with the end of his pencil, wondering when Mike and Rabbi Norton got so friendly. Mike is already praying and doing all this religious stuff...maybe that's why they're tight and all.

"Okay, thank you, Rabbi Norton," he hears Mike say.

"What did Rabbi Norton tell you? You saying all of it?"

"No. Um, Jeremy? Can I borrow a hat?"

"Yeah, sure."

Mike passes by Jeremy on his way to the closet. "Homework?"

"I got a couple term papers coming. You, too, by the way — I asked your classmates."

"Not due until Monday."

"Yeah, but I don't have the weekend."

"Right, the presentation on Sunday."

"And on Saturday I'm —"

"I know. But the professors don't seem to mind when I give anything in late."

"That's because it's always better than anyone else's."

"I don't do that on purpose, you know."

"Yeah, I hear you. But Mike, you didn't give me a chance to finish up what I was trying to tell you."

"Hmm?" asks Mike, plopping himself down on his bed and adjusting the pilot hat more firmly on his head.

"I know I said I was coming this week with you to the rabbi's, but I've got to back out of it."

"Huh?"

"I've got something going on with Cole."

"But Jeremy...it's Shabbos."

"Yeah? So? I mean, give me a break. This whole Shabbos thing is fun and I love it and all, but unlike some people around here, I have a life outside of Rabbi Norton's world. And let's get real here — it's not as if I keep Shabbos when I'm not spending it with him."

"But Jeremy...I thought...I mean, every Shabbos counts. And Cole can wait. All through life, there will always be enough boneheads out there to make you happy. But spending a Shabbos with Rabbi Norton —"

"Maybe I WOULD rather spend my day hanging out with Cole,

okay? Cole is my friend — but maybe that concept is too hard for you to understand. And sheesh, Mike, since when did you become the voice of conscience?"

"WE'RE friends," says Mike.

"Are we?"

Mike bites his bottom lip and stares at the cover of his siddur.

"Aaw, man...I'm sorry. I was just...I haven't been spending an awful lot of time with Cole these days, what with getting everything ready for filming this summer and the presentation and stuff. And I don't see how this Judaism is fitting into my plans. It's not all that practical for me at this stage in my life, you know what I'm saying? Like, I'm glad it worked for you and all, and it's been real for me, too, but...when it boils down to it, I can't turn my whole life upside-down for it. So you go, have fun, yo? And tell me about it when you get back."

"But Jeremy, it IS for you. How can you say that when you've got the truth about life thrown into your face?"

"I'm not going, Mike, alright? Discussion over."

Mike sighs and flips his siddur opens to the correct place, his mind working overtime to explore the options. He hopes Hashem will help out with this, because he is out of ideas.

■ ■ ■

"Hello? Anyone home?" Jeremy says, peeping his head between the screen door and the door frame.

"In the kitchen!" calls Mrs. Norton.

Jeremy kicks off his shoes in the entranceway, then makes his way down the hallway, energetically swinging his legs forward. Mrs. Norton is stirring something on the stove.

"Oh, hello, Jeremy. Rabbi Norton is in his study right now. He should be out soon, though, when the Cohens arrive. Unless you need to speak to him now...?"

"No, it's okay. I just thought I'd tell you that, thanks for the invitation, but, yeah, I can't make it this Shabbos."

"Oh?" says Mrs. Norton. "The boys will be so disappointed."

"Yeah...I just have a lot of work to do — year's almost over and stuff, y'know?"

"So, *nu*? Shabbos is not for another five hours. Maybe you can get enough done by then. You never know — can you reach that bowl for me? Thank you — maybe one of the Cohen boys can come over later to your dorm and help out. They're very intelligent, you know."

"No, no. That's okay. Really."

"...It's not the work, is it, Jeremy?"

"Yes. I mean, no. It's more like —"

"Sit down and tell me while I finish with this potato kugel. I want to hear what's going on in that *kupple* of yours."

Jeremy sits down on the edge of a seat and scuffs the toe of his shoe against the floor. "Thing is," he says, "I got a bit of a thing to go to this Saturday, you know? It's been a while since I've gotten to hang out with my friends, drink a couple beers — potato kugel?"

"Potato kugel. Shabbos wouldn't be the same without it. Why don't you spend time with these friends of yours on Sunday?"

"I've got a presentation on Sunday. Tell me, have you ever tried…" Jeremy gets up, rummages through the contents of the spice drawer, and comes back with an armful of shakers. "Here. Can I try…?"

"*Gesuntaheit.*" Mrs. Norton steps back from the bowl and carries three onions to the garbage to peel. "You know your way around the kitchen?"

"Yeah, it's kind of my hobby… I don't go around announcing it and all, you get what I'm saying, but…see, I always used to cook for my family growing up down under. My mother, she, she wasn't like you. She never…felt well enough to cook us meals. So I taught myself. I wasn't stupid. Obviously. And I got good at it. I liked it. Then I come to America, and it's just not as macho as it was back home, where I would just pull out the old barbeque for my friends and someone would bring the beer and we'd all just hang out."

"I don't know much about what's cool or not, but I should think that men like a barbeque here as much as men anywhere. My husband loves to do it summers for the *kehillah*."

"Ahum…no one's ever mentioned something like it with the guys. I assume that means it's not exactly something acceptable. Better not to risk it, don't you think?"

"Is being this 'cool person' *that* important to you, Jeremy?"

"Wha — I mean, yeah. When you put it like that, it's kind of hard to answer, but, like, being cool's just something you are. And if you're cool, you're a happening person. Things go smoother, you know? People go after you instead of you having to go looking for friends. People listen to you, and, like, people think you're cool."

"I'm not sure I understand all these politics. I just feel that friends should like the you that is you, and if they don't, then they don't really like you. People that don't like you aren't your friends, so… Nu, maybe there are things I don't understand."

Jeremy looked thoughtful. "No, I get how it could work in your community. I see all these unlikely people together like Lem and Dan. But things are different where I'm coming from."

"Well, either way, you come over and make potato kugel any time you feel like it. I won't complain," Mrs. Norton declares.

Jeremy chuckles. "What do you still have left to make for Shabbos?"

"What do I still have left? There's always something left to do for Shabbos…schnitzel — that's what I still need done. I should have made it last night. I don't know why I left it for the last minute."

"That breaded chicken?"

"That's the one."

"Awright. Where is the meaty counter and stuff?"

Rabbi Norton chooses to enter the kitchen at that moment. His eyes rest on Jeremy and his face lights up. "Ah, Jeremy," he says, "you're joining us this Shabbos, right?"

"Uh…of course!" says Jeremy, a flush rising over his face.

Rabbi Norton nods happily. Mrs. Norton shakes her head slightly, wondering how her husband has managed to accomplish, with just one simple question, what she had been trying to do all this time. Perhaps Jeremy had wanted to come all the while. Perhaps all he'd needed was that little push.

Perhaps.

■ ■ ■

Rob pauses his game as Gordon and Ben step off the platform elevator. The carpet rolls over the opening, and they stand there, facing him in weary expectation.

Rob leans back in his bright-red leather armchair. "Ben! Gordon! Come, sit down quick. QUICK! It's so exciting!"

Ben sits down on a chair on the other side of Rob's desk, his hands gripping his knees with cautious anticipation. Gordon takes his place in the chair next to Ben's, glancing swiftly at his wristwatch.

"It's about the missing money," says Rob, smirking in self-satisfaction.

"You mean Maxcom?" asks Ben, yanking at his cuffs.

Rob looks up with a slightly quizzical expression. "Kind of."

"Well, in that case, I have a bit of a confession to make."

Gordon looks sideways at Ben, eyebrows raised.

"It's my son —"

"Yes, that's what I called you up to talk about, in a way. Mike definitely helped a lot with this."

"No, not Mike. Chad."

"But Chad has nothing to do with this."

"Yes. Yes, he does. I'm afraid I've…I've discovered that he is the, uh, mole."

"What?!" Gordon practically screams, eyes bulging.

"I thought we already established that a while back," says Rob, shrugging and twirling a ballpoint pen around his finger.

Ben had been eyeing his pant creases, but now his head snaps up. "Huh? No Rob, we didn't. And I'll do something about this. Really, I am so sorry."

"For what? You're not making much sense, Ben. You told me the other day you'd found out about the mole and Maxcom."

"About, Rob, not who."

"Oh," says Rob, blinking once.

Gordon's eyes spin in frustration. "Wait a second. If you knew Chad was giving away information, then why didn't you do something about it?!"

"Because I told him to do it. Duh." Rob rolls his eyes.

"Why would you do something like that?" asks Gordon, hysterical exasperation straining his voice.

"Well, this way Maxcom thought they were getting the information, and Chad wasn't giving them anything at all."

"Sure was something," mutters Ben.

"No, actually," says Rob, "there are so many production and technical flaws in those product plans he gave them...my, my, what angry customers Maxcom has to deal with these days! Anyway, Chad helped put them off the scent of my new project...until he quit. That was the pits. I had to speed up production tenfold..."

"Maxcom's knock-offs don't work properly?" asks Gordon in a significantly subdued tone of voice.

"It's true," says Ben. "I meant to tell you...I didn't realize why, though."

"I don't believe this," says Gordon, shaking his head wildly. "No, no, it's too much."

But Ben has taken it all in stride. He faces Rob head-on. "Put Maxcom off the scent of what?"

"Oh, that's what I wanted to talk to you about. My new idea. It was very expensive, but it's done now, and I know it's going to be really, really, really popular. Mike helped a whole bunch, you know. It was taking us forever and ever, and he finally e-mails me to say it's ready."

"What?" asks Ben, wondering what has been going on in his family right under his very nose.

"A whole new trail to be blazed. It's a video game."

Gordon smacks his forehead to the palm of his hand.

"No, don't be like that, Gordon. It's not just a video game. It's a whole new approach to virtual reality gaming systems. Once you put on that headset, you've got 360° vision and sounds come from where they look like they're coming from...you're in a whole different world!"

"And my son built this?" asks Ben in disbelief.

"Partly. He was doing it anyway...something for school. He offered to help in exchange for some stocks in the final product. I figured I'd put him in charge of the whole thing when it was finished, but he tells me he wants to concentrate on other studies... you know what I'm talking about, Ben, right? Or did he tell me not to tell you? Can't remember... But anyway, since he won't be heading all this, I will."

"But, but, Rob! You can't be so concentrated on one thing. You've got a whole company to run. What about all the other projects?" asks Ben, forehead creased.

"Well, you two have been managing quite nicely without me until now."

Ben attempts a half-hearted protest, which Rob waves away impatiently.

"I think it's time it became official. From now on, you two are in charge of all those things. My department will move into this building and you'll set up main headquarters in that office building off Dudley Square."

"It's too late," Gordon moans, too shocked to concentrate on the main point at hand, instead nitpicking on a minor detail. "It's sold. I checked it out."

"Of course it's been sold," says Rob, rolling his eyes. He reaches into his top desk drawer and pulls out a document, which he slaps onto the table with thrilled finesse.

"You bought it?"

"You did ask me to, didn't you?"

"I can't believe it!" A huge smile breaks over Gordon's face.

"What I can't believe is that I'm officially in charge!" says Ben. "You sure about this, Rob?"

"Oh, yeah. I never did like all that pressure I was under, being on top."

Pressure? thinks Ben.

"This is much more fun." Rob crosses his legs up onto his desk in satisfied calmness.

"Rob?" asks Gordon.

"Yup. That's my name. Don't wear it out."

"Well, seeing as we're having this building and all, and we're moving out...can I ask you for a sort of present?"

"I gave you a building. I don't want to spoil you now."

"I meant, can you answer a question? Just one."

"Yup. Okay, I answered it. We're done here."

"Seriously."

"Yes, sure, Gordon. Ask away."

"The 'v-lator.' Why won't you market it? I mean — it hardly uses any electricity, it's economical, it's fast, it doesn't damage the environment, it's sleek...all the good stuff everyone wants to hear. We could make millions."

"Yes, we could. But it's quite simple," says Rob. "I haven't the faintest idea how I built it. It was a bit of a fluke and I couldn't do it again if I tried."

Later, taking the elevator platform back down to floor 60, Ben looks over at Gordon and says, "I told you he wasn't an idiot."

CHAPTER 14
NO FAIRYTALE ENDING

The *Havdalah* candle hisses angrily as its flame is forcibly drowned in a puddle of wine.

"A *gutte vach*, a *mazeldike vach*!" says Frumma, two seconds ahead of everyone else.

The Cohens hurry out to their van.

"Take care, Minna!" calls Frumma. "See you next week. Will Etty be home then?"

"No, her high school finishes in June."

"Well, I found that daughter of yours a summer job. Tell her to call me." Frumma hoists herself into the passenger seat of the van.

Zev shakes Rabbi Norton's hand, then Mike's. He stops at Jeremy and eyes him for a moment before enveloping him in a bear hug. "I've got enough boys of my own," he says in a voice only audible to Jeremy, "to know something's bothering you. Whatever it is, I hope it sorts itself out. And I hope to see you again soon." He squeezes Jeremy as though he means to crush something within himself into Jeremy's soul.

Jeremy nods and Zev gets into his van, tooting his horn as he pulls out of the driveway, with Rachel blowing kisses to everyone from the back seat.

Tzvi, Yanky, and Mrs. Norton head across the street for home. Rabbi Norton steers Mike and Jeremy into the shul.

The kitchen seems cold and empty in the dark, but Rabbi Norton flicks the light switch on and waves the boys toward the table. "Sit down, sit down," he says. "Let's have a bit of *melaveh malkah* before you go. Coffee?"

"Yes, please," says Mike softly, resting the back of his head against his chair and smiling peacefully.

"Yeah, why not?" says Jeremy, pressing his chin on the table top.

Rabbi Norton stirs instant coffee into three mugs with a spoon, then clinks the spoon against the side of the sink before dropping it in.

"Well, boys, what did you think of this Shabbos? It's the last one before exams hit you."

"Ah, don't remind me about those," groans Jeremy.

"I liked the discussion about elevating the *gashmiyus* into *ruchniyus*," says Mike, blowing gently on his coffee. "That concept gives everything meaning." Then he says a *shehakol* slowly and carefully before taking a sip.

"And you, Jeremy? What did you take out of this Shabbos?"

"Potato kugel."

"Yes, it was delicious, I must agree."

Jeremy sighs and he looks up at Rabbi Norton with a pained expression on his face. "You want to hear the truth?" His voice rises to a sarcastic, squealing falsetto: "I liked the discussion about elevating the *gashmi* —?" Jeremy yanks at his hair in frustration. "Yeah, I mean, I loved it. I always love Shabbos here. But it's, like, here's Mike, it's one year, and all of a sudden, he's a completely different person, and I can't change at all. It's not that I don't get what you're telling us, because I do, but it's, like, everyone is expecting me to become religious, but...before I knew about all this religious stuff, I was happy with my life. I wasn't like Mike, searching for answers.

"I mean, I'm not trying to brag or anything, but I'm an incredibly famous rising director in the entertainment industry. Things are going really great for me. And as much as I love all this Jewishness, it's not easy, okay? It conflicts with everything I've ever wanted out of life.

"And then suddenly I'm finding out about G-d, and Torah, and *mitzvos*, and it's like there's so much more. But it's hard. Too hard. I just don't see myself doing this. I'm sorry. I don't want to waste any more of your time. Find someone else. Change their world. And thank you."

"Jeremy, come. No one's expecting you to turn yourself around overnight. It's enough that you come for Shabbos."

"No. It's not enough. There's nothing worse than feeling like a hypocrite. See you around." He leaves through the back door, letting it slam behind him.

Mike stands up to follow him, but Rabbi Norton reaches out and presses down on his shoulder. "Let him go. He needs to be alone for a while."

Mike nods and settles himself back down. "But you'll talk to him, right? You'll make him understand?"

"Mike, I can't make him do anything. One can try and explain, but ultimately, the final decision is left up to the person himself. Come, there's nothing to be done right now. Let's learn something."

■ ■ ■

Mike finds within himself a membrane of peace that reaches out to surround him. It's a sort of euphoria a person will sometimes feel, a foolish feeling of being untouchably high and free, that usually doesn't last more than seconds after being discovered within the person.

He'd never walked. Didn't much like it; speed was what he'd been after. Cold, rushing speed that hurtles the mind into a blurred, gripping flight. Yet now he finds himself walking idly along the road, hands jammed into his pants pockets in casual relaxation.

Then, from somewhere in his mind, comes a flash of pain and aggravation. If only Jeremy could understand. He wishes he could share this feeling with him, the calmness of Torah that channels all that loose, pulling energy. He knows Rabbi Norton told him to give Jeremy time. He understands. But it's been a few hours. Maybe they could go for a drive. Go down to the cliff line and watch the sunrise.

He smiles to himself as he walks through the parking lot on his way to the dorm, but his smile freezes as his gaze passes over the corner where he normally parks his car. It's not there.

"Hey," he says, latching his fingers into the belt loop of a passing sophomore student, dragging him back. "My car…? You know where it's gone?"

"Oh, hey, man. Good to see you. Actually, I heard that your brother and Cole were talking, right? And they went into your room. Came out with your car keys. Man, I can't believe you let Cole use your car. It's all over campus…everyone knows you hate the dude. Then I'm figuring, right, hey, his brother's along to keep an eye on things."

"Cole and my brother?"

"Yo! The whole bunch of knuckleheads left, like, a few hours ago. Random… You coming tonight? Omega Delta? I'm acting D.J. It's gonna be rocking, man."

Mike shrugs. "Not really."

"Wha-what else happening?"

"Sleep. Sleep is happening."

"I hear you. Yeah, I heard the professors talking and all…purely accidental, yo."

"Purely accidental."

"Right, and they're going on about this new computer thing you've got going. They say it's revolutionary and all that jazz. Keep it up, man. Get some rest."

"See you."

This conversation has been extremely disconcerting, perhaps

the most disconcerting factor of it being that Mike had felt the rising of excitement at the mention of the party. What was the matter with him? He was different now. Partying was a waste of time, something from his juvenile past. There were far more important and more meaningful things to life.

He enters his dorm room quietly. "Hey," he whispers into the dark.

"Hey, yourself," comes the response.

Mike tosses himself backwards onto his bed. "It's happening at Omega Delta."

"Wanna go?"

"I dunno…"

"Mike."

"Hmmm?"

"Let's go for a drive. Like we used to… Watch the sunrise over the cliff line. Please."

"I can't."

"Alright. I get it."

"No, I would. But Chad took my car for Cole and his robotic dolts."

"Chad and Cole?"

"That's what I heard."

"That is very disturbing."

"Yeah."

"You let them take your car?"

"No."

They both lie on their backs, staring up at the ceiling. Silence settles around them. Somewhere off in the distance they hear someone yell. A car door slams below the window.

"Let's walk then," says Jeremy.

"Okay." Mike rolls himself out of bed.

The walk is not as far as Jeremy remembers, but it is a lot further than Mike does.

They settle into their respective positions. Jeremy's feet dangle over the edge of the cliff. Mike folds his feet under his legs and wraps his arms around himself.

"Chilly," says Jeremy.

"Yup," says Mike.

And there is nothing much else to say. They sit uncomfortably side by side, the unspoken words that need to be said hanging between them like a pressing itch. The feeling creeps into tense nerves and stretches and yanks at them like pins and needles. Jeremy fidgets.

"Know what time the sun's coming up today?" he asks finally.

"Um, I dunno... It's the end of May, right?"

"Mmm-hmm."

"Then... —" Mike checks his cell phone's clock — "should be soon-ish." As if on cue, some of the sky's midnight ink washes away.

Jeremy squints into the chasm below. "Car's gone," he says.

"Oh. Yeah." A small smile presses Mike's chin upwards.

"That was a crazy night."

"This one or then?"

"Both."

"I won't argue."

"Nope."

"I can't believe I did that."

"You're odd."

"It didn't seem odd at the time."

"I always kind of wondered what the thought process was behind that one."

"I was trying to...you know."

"Evidently not."

"I wanted to touch the sunrise. I thought if I could...whatever. I know it sounds weird now."

"...Touch the sunrise, huh?"

"I missed."

"Only by a little."

"Heh."

After a pause, Jeremy perks up. "Say, you know, if you really want to, there could be a way to reach it."

"How's that? Rocket-ship?"

"Naaw. Not as practical. But if you fill up the chasm below with water, you could swim to it."

"And you say I'm odd." Mike rolls his eyes slightly, a smile stretching the left side of his face. And yet, a strange and thoughtful expression crosses his countenance as something of what has just been said hits him.

"Yeah, my mind's a lot more dramatic than I am most of the time."

"Your mind is an extremely scary place."

"I wouldn't talk."

"And yet you do."

"Ha ha, very funny."

"It was."

"Mike?"

"What?"

"Sorry for this whole Shabbos, yeah? I didn't mean to explode like that. I usually try to keep things real...it kind of got out of hand."

"But what was said...did you mean it?"

"Yeah. Sorry."

"I guess there's not much to say then."

"Nope... Man, you sure know how to make a fellow feel good about himself. C'mon, let me off the hook. Don't look like that."

"Like what?"

"Like that!"

"You mean like Mike?"

"You know what I mean."

"...I can't let you off the hook. You know that. You don't even want me to. Now be quiet and watch the sunrise."

"Oh, right. That. When did it start?"

■ ■ ■

"Omig-d! Omig-d!" the girl screams, slumping against the brick wall of the dorm. Her eyes are unnaturally large and her body shakes and trembles. "Omig-d! Omig-d!" she keeps screaming. Next to her, her friend crumples onto the ground, pressing her face against the bricks, shrieking in short gasps.

Windows open; tired heads peep out above them. Early risers surround them.

"What happened?" someone asks, kneeling in front of them.

"Omig-d, Omig-d, it happened like THREE INCHES from me!" she screeches, clawing at her hair. "I can't, I can't," she wails.

"Shhh, calm down...take a deep breath. Shhh, shhh."

"The car...it...it went right through the bus stop. The driver didn't even press on the brakes."

"That's horrible."

"I know," she bawls. "It was Mike Burns' car."

"No."

"It just went through the bus stop. He didn't even press the brakes. He. Just. Went. Through. HE JUST WENT THROUGH!"

It is around this time that Mike and Jeremy return to the campus and pick their way through the crowd.

"Whoa," says Jeremy. "What's goin' on, people?"

The girl who has been sobbing against the wall looks up, face streaked with mascara-colored tears. "Mike?" she asks, her voice cracking.

"Oh, uh, hi, Jamie. What's..."

"You're safe." A smile bursts across her face, and she swipes her eyes with the back of her hand.

"Um, yeah, I guess..." Mike's mind falls into muddled confusion.

"But your car, I saw it. It went right through the bus stop."

"What?"

"Just before... Are you hurt?"

Mike's face pales. "Chad," he says and turns in a whirl, using his elbows to shove curious people out of his way as he runs. Jeremy stands in place, stunned for a time, and then stumbles hurriedly after him.

The bus stop is two blocks down. An ambulance passes by them going in the opposite direction. Its lights are off; it is silent, dead.

Up ahead at the bus stop is a mangled twist of cheap black metal, plastic, and splintered glass, the front of Mike's car slammed into the back, held somehow midair, mid-flight. The hood is crumpled like a wrinkled cherry-red elephant. The front window is smashed in, and all around are gaping teeth of glass with cracks that spider out in frighteningly beautiful patterns. Below the strips of yellow police tape, the pavement is stained in rusty red splotches. Jeremy feels slightly sick.

The world shifts a step to the left of Mike, and he reaches out an arm, smacking it into a passing police officer.

"Move it, kid; this is an accident scene," the police officer says, clamping meaty hands on Mike's shoulders and giving him a gentle push in the direction of the other side of the road.

Mike looks back at the officer with a hopeless expression on his face. "Please," he says, "the people in the car…" but the officer is already on to something else.

Jeremy chases after the officer and faces him head-on. He talks animatedly with him for a minute or so, nodding calmly. The officer laughs at something he says. Finally, Jeremy turns towards Mike, who sits on the shoulder of the road, a blank expression on his face. He walks over to him and tugs him up by the arms.

"Come on, Mike," he says, "let's get back to the dorm."

Mike follows limply, blindly. "Chad," he says in a hollow voice. "What did he say…?"

"Um," says Jeremy, blinking and regarding Mike cautiously. "Um," he says again. "Maybe we should get back to the dorm first."

Mike sits down stubbornly in the middle of a puddle, oblivious to the water seeping through his clothing. "Where's Chad? Is he hurt? I want to go to him."

"Aah…haha. Aw, man, I can't….." Jeremy rubs the back of his neck awkwardly, not meeting Mike's eyes. "The accident was pretty serious."

Mike looks up at him desperately.

"It looks like they were drunk…they drove straight through. Mike…um… they're…it was a very bad crash…they weren't wearing seatbelts. Um, they, they…when the ambulance came, there wasn't anything they could do. They're kind of all…dead."

Mike stares forward in shock, the words almost hitting him, but not quite. "No," he says in firm conviction. "It can't be. Chad always wears his seatbelt."

Jeremy doesn't know where to look or what to do with himself.

"Chad," Mike whispers.

He flies away, his feet moving on their own accord. He cannot feel them; he cannot breathe; he is disconnected. How could this…? Why…? No. No.

Not Chad.

Please.

Why?

Chad.

No.

It's not fair.

The stairs lurch in a sickening plunge as he staggers up them and into his dorm room. The bed, his bed…it bounces and surrounds him like a sponge. The world is a muffled silence; he cannot hear a thing.

Chad couldn't be.

He presses his face into the cool pillow, not feeling anything but a floating sensation.

How could it be? Not Chad. Why?

Why…?

All those words he meant to one day say, all those days they'd spent together, all that he'd thought would always be.

Gone.

It's too late.

No.

He couldn't be gone. Not yet. Not now. He'd just been with him yesterday. He was supposed to always be there. He was supposed to be there forever.

Chad.

But he wasn't here anymore. Chad was gone. He would never, ever see him again.

A squeezing sob rises up in his throat behind his nose and presses into his eyes. His heart aches like it wishes to leave him. He doesn't understand.

If he'd been in his dorm room, he wouldn't have given them his keys.

He squirms his face against his pillow and gathers his knees to his chest.

No. No.

An awful sinking feeling washes every nerve in his body, tearing his body apart from the inside out. He stays curled up in a ball. The tugging grief will never leave him.

His fists clutch the wrinkled sheets below him in a weak grip. His eyes open, and he looks upwards, his tongue thick.

From this angle, the coffee cup is foremost in his vision, and a fresh lurch of painful despair fills him.

He rolls slowly from his bed and crouches by his bedside, reaching for the coffee cup and holding it tenderly in his hands.

"Chad," he says aloud, as the warmth of the cup seeps into his numbed fingers.

He sits and holds it for a time, and then a strange expression slides down his face. His throat catches.

Dazed, he leaves the room and exits the dorm, heading towards the freshmen dorm, the fresh cup of coffee held loosely in hands that have lost life. Around him in the fields and doorways are students. Some cry, some hug, some gossip, some don't seem to care at all.

In his dorm room, Chad stretches out from his stiff, perfect posture, and is startled to find the door opening. He clucks his tongue in impatient irritancy.

"Michael?" he says to the huddled figure at his door.

Mike stands there and holds out his coffee cup to Chad.

Chad?

Chad is here.

Alive.

How?

"You've certainly gotten an early start to your day. What prompted this?"

Mike shoves his steaming coffee cup at Chad.

"So put ice cubes in it. They don't sell them cold, you know... Really, you must learn to be more self-sufficient."

Mike lowers his head to stare at the carpet fibers below his feet.

"Oh, before I forget, I lent Cole your car keys. He thanks you again for your generous offer. Yes, and that is all."

Mike opens his mouth as though he wishes to say something, but all that comes out is a gasp of air. He reaches out an arm as if he means to embrace Chad.

"I'm sorry, Michael, but I am extraordinarily busy this morning, and I must ask you to leave. Not that I don't enjoy your company, but work before play. Good day."

Mike seems to half swoon out the door. He doesn't say a word.

■ ■ ■

Jeremy sits on his bed, calmly going through his exam schedule. Somewhere in his mind, he understands that he shouldn't be doing this. He should be upset. Extremely upset. His friends, all his friends — they just died. He knows that, but it just doesn't seem to sink in.

He looks out the window and wonders distractedly what he should do for lunch.

Suddenly, something hits him in the pit of his stomach. He had been planning on going with them that Saturday! Beer and stuff, Cole had said... He, Jeremy, could have died.

Nothing fancy. A peanut butter sandwich, maybe.

CHAPTER 15
SO LONG AND FAREWELL

"Claire, what's this?"

Claire bustles around the kitchen, moving objects around unnecessarily and fussing over Rob. Ben tails her, flapping a scrap of paper at her retreating back.

"Claire, what is it?"

Claire bends her head down close to Rob, who sits at the table concentrating all his attention on gathering the last scraps of ravioli onto the left tine of his fork. "Rob, honey, can I offer you more of anything?"

He looks up at her, tapping his fork against the edge of his plate. "Um, actually — "

"Claire, will you answer me, please?!" Ben thumps his palms down on the table on the other side of Rob.

Claire stubbornly lifts her chin, avoiding Ben's

gaze. "I think it's pretty self-apparent as to what it is, BEN." The name "Ben" snaps off the end of her tongue, like an insult.

Ben's forehead darkens. Rob tries to shrink into his seat.

"Yeah, actually, it is, thanks." Ben folds his arms, feet apart in a power stance. "I understand what it is perfectly. What I don't understand is WHY it is. I believe I told you that we are not getting the court involved."

"And I believe I said that I was."

There is a silence so heavy it seems to press out all life in the room. In the hanging, dangling silence, the two stare at each other.

Rob melts off the edge of his seat and makes a quick escape to the living room. Neither Claire nor Ben notices.

Claire is first at attempting to break the impasse. She turns angrily towards the counter, leaning against the cold granite and glaring out the window, arms folded and lower lip jutting out to prevent it from trembling.

"People like that man should not be allowed to roam free," she says in a voice so filled with burning hatred that Ben takes an involuntarily step backwards. "Preying on vulnerable children when they're so far away from home..." Her voice becomes wistful and sad. "Playing on my...," her voice cracks, "on my baby's feelings. You don't understand, Ben. No, you don't understand at all. I tried so hard to bring my children up properly and yet... nothing ever seemed to go right with Mike. But I tried as much as I could. I let him go to college because I thought that was the best thing for him, and now...look what happened. That beast took my son's reasoning entirely out of my reach and there's nothing for me to do for him anymore." Her voice is high and quiet. Teardrops slip off the end of her nose and fall to the countertop. She does nothing to stop them.

Ben sighs and moves closer to his wife.

She pulls away and faces him, eyes smoldering. "And YOU! You don't even CARE," she hisses in a loaded whisper.

Ben retreats a few steps, holding his hands up in surrender, suddenly feeling very tired. There is another long silence. He rubs the flesh between his eyebrows. Finally he looks up at her, and his eyes seem to mirror her pain.

"Don't think this isn't hard for me, too. Why shouldn't it be? I sent my son off to college hoping he'll somehow sort himself out there and come back ready to help me in the business. Next thing I know, he comes back — a different person.

"I don't like… Claire, you KNOW I don't like surprises, and heaven knows…a surprise like that… But you know what? I thought about it for a long time, and I realized that as much as I am disturbed by the sudden change, it was a change for the best. What are we suing the rabbi for? Straightening my kid out?"

"Let me worry about what I'm suing him for." Her voice cuts him.

Ben looks down to the side and his lips form a stubborn grimace as he takes a deep breath. "No, Claire. I won't allow it. This has gone far enough."

Her eyes snap upwards to meet his in defiance, a "don't-you-dare" expression on her face.

"I'm sorry." He meets her eyes in deep conviction. "I am still your husband, and I put my foot down; it ends right now."

He turns away from her and walks out of the kitchen, feeling the piercing bullets of Claire's anger aimed at his back.

Claire remains frozen in her place, hands shaking in undisguised fury. How dare he. How DARE he.

She stalks to the table and noisily stacks the plates together, not bothering to be gentle with her delicate china. Dumping the dishes into the sink, she strains her ears, trying to locate the source of a video game's sounds. The lounge.

She abandons the kitchen and makes her way to the lounge.

"Rob?" Her voice is piercing, commanding. Hunched over his joystick, Rob moves his game character into a critical stage.

"Argh!" Claire screams, beginning to pace behind him. "My husband is being absolutely INSANE. He won't help me, and I…I don't even know what to do anymore! What should I do? I have to do SOMETHING, Rob!"

"Hmm…"

"I've got to save my son. Oh!" she wails. "Rob, you'll help me, won't you?"

"No," says Rob, machine-gunning down some innocent looking fluff-balls on the screen.

"What?" Claire's eyes widen, her heart jumping. She stops in her place. "Rob?"

"No, I won't help you, Claire." Here Rob pauses the game, putting his joystick down carefully on the coffee table. "And that is because you are being ridiculous."

"What are you — "

"I've gotten to know Mike a lot better than most people, Claire, as you know. Now, you...," Rob reaches into the bowl of nuts on the coffee table and pops a fistful of cashews into his mouth, chewing thoughtfully, "you're acting like somebody died, when what really happened is he actually began to live." Wiping some crumbs off his lap, Rob gets up and leaves the room.

Claire slumps down onto the sofa, rubbing behind her ears, brows knitted in disturbance. She hears the front door open, and lifts her head. "ROB!" she screams. "What do you mean, Rob? Rob, get back in here, get back in here NOW!" But the front door clicks shut.

As she hears Rob's motorcycle roar out of their driveway, a shiver runs through her. They've betrayed her.

Everyone.

Quite suddenly, she feels very, very cold.

■ ■ ■

It's four o' clock in the morning. Exams are over, and Mike sits on his bed, legs pulled up to his chest, watching Jeremy's back rise and fall.

So much has happened.

Too much has happened.

It was like life piled up into one weekend, a never-ending roller-coaster of nerves and grief.

He probably flunked every exam.

He looks down at the ticket clutched in his hand. Months ago, he'd overheard a conversation. He hadn't meant to, but... Someone had said, *"Just make up your mind already. What do you want out of life?"* It had seemed odd to him then. Wasn't it obvious that what you want out of life is what life is for? So he'd thought about it and realized that really, even if you do know better, that doesn't mean anything. Otherwise, he'd be eating bran flakes and spinach-alfalfa salad every morning with Vergil.

He folds up his blanket and places it at the foot of his bed. Chad will take home everything he leaves here. He can count on Chad for that, like he can count on Chad for everything. Like he's always counted on him.

When he'd thought that Chad was dead, he'd…he'd…

And Chad will never know. He'll never understand what Mike had felt in that sickening hour, when it seemed as though…

Mike can't ever tell him.

Mike walks over to Jeremy's bed. He reaches out his hand and softly strokes Jeremy's ear. Jeremy moans and swats at him in his sleep. Mike smiles, but he really wants to cry.

He doesn't want to.

He can't.

Why does everything have to change?

There are too many things that will be different, too many new people.

But he can't rely on Jeremy anymore. Jeremy is not with him.

And he can't rely on Chad anymore. Chad can't always be there.

He has to learn how to get by on his own.

Just make up your mind already. What do you want out of life?

He looks down at Jeremy and hitches his school bag higher on his back. He knows the answer.

Potato kugel.

EPILOGUE

The afternoon is winding down as he makes his way through the cobbled stones of Yerushalayim. A cool glass of water is on his mind as he takes the stairs to his apartment, the spring in his step following upwards into his slight frame.

His wife calls to him from the kitchen; he has a visitor in the living room waiting for him, can he please go in, and how was work today and learning, was it good, and would he like a glass of water.

He answers yes.

He enters the living room, his eyes gazing about him in intelligent, yet innocent, almost childlike, curiosity. They stop upon reaching the face of the visitor.

"Jeremy?" he asks, although he knows exactly who it is.

"Hey, buddy, howzit going?"

"Wow, I haven't seen you in quite a while, have I? Are you here to do shots for another project?" Michoel sits down on the sofa facing him.

"No. Not really."

"No? A visit then?"

"Kind of." Jeremy looks up and meets Michoel's eyes from below an unruly mess of curls with hesitant pride. He awkwardly raises a hand and adjusts his knitted *kippah*.

Michoel notices the movement, and his eyebrows raise slightly. "When did this…?" he gestures with an open palm at Jeremy.

"You mean the *kippah* situation?"

"Yes, the, uh…the, uh…the situation."

"Been going on for, oh, about a couple months, actually."

Michoel nods.

"Yeah…" says Jeremy, smiling down at his sandaled feet in sheepish excitement.

Michoel fiddles with a cuff button.

"Abba!" comes a high-pitched voice attached to Michoel's five-year-old son. "Abba, look what I made in school!" He runs into the room, holding a *parshah* arts-and-crafts proudly above his head.

"Wow!" says Michoel, a quiet smile slipping sideways onto his face. "It's so nice. Good, good job." He reaches out a fumbling hand and awkwardly pats his son on the head. They share a special smile together.

"I'm the best cutter. You forgot to say I'm the best cutter, Abba."

"You're the best cutter ever. A million times a better cutter than I was in pre-grade one."

"A lot better than I am NOW," says Jeremy.

The boy turns to face Jeremy with a puzzled smile.

"Hey. Remember me?"

The boy shakes his head shyly.

"Naaw. You were just a baby last time I came, weren't you? I'm Jeremy."

The boy shrugs and dashes out of the room.

Jeremy leans his head back against the sofa. He sighs wearily and looks up at the low ceiling for inspiration. It reminds him of cottage cheese. He groans and bangs his head against the back of the sofa, and tears spring to his eyes.

"Jeremy?"

"Yeah, I know. It's just...I wish I would have... Y'know, ten years ago, we both were in the same place. Now look at you. You've got an apartment, a wife, kids. You learn like a regular *kollel* person. You're a totally different person, and you've got just...the most amazing things going for you.

"And me — what have I got? A couple awards...some trophy statues with eyes more alive than mine are..." Jeremy hangs his head between his knees, then lifts it, scrubbing his face with the palms of his hands. He kicks out at the coffee table with a sandaled foot. "The entertainment industry ain't all Disneyland, what can I tell you, buddy. It's a dirty business. You get caught up in it, and everyone's making like you're the big-shot. You're center of the world. It's like quicksand.

"And then one day I wake up and I think to myself — how did I get to this? How did I fall so low so fast? Didn't even know how it happened.

"One day I was all 'I'm gonna change the world,' and next thing I knew, I was playing their game. I was giving them what they wanted. I was just another Hollywood director…"

"So I left."

"Just like that?"

"Juuuuuuuuuuust like that. Yup. Just. Like. That. No, not really… It was kind of more of a process. Actually, um…I haven't officially left, but…"

Mike smiles down at his fingertips.

"I will, okay? I'm telling you! I'm gonna. I know already, it's time for me to grow up…I get it. Hey, I always was a late bloomer, y'know? So I'm gonna do this thing. Probably. Just watch. Yeah… No, because you made it look easy, and let me tell you, it's not."

"No, it's not. It wasn't."

"No?"

"No."

"Yeah, but you did it."

"It's not a contest. You're my friend, Jeremy."

"Are we friends?" Jeremy quips.

Mike gives him a look. A look like he's going to laugh. A look like he's going to cry.

" Okay, fine...because I'm not exactly religious. I'm kind of taking this whole deal slow, y'know? Testing the waters. But you never know. Maybe one day...."

There is a cooling, melting silence hanging between them. The clock ticks softly into the air. An insect buzzes off by the window, and then sound ceases for a moment.

"Maybe," Michoel finally says, his voice scratchy and low.

■ ■ ■

"...an' then, an' then, he even said I could! So hahaha on her. Because really, my Abba knows more."

Ben chuckles over the phone line. "That's right! But next week you won't be at her house, because guess what, Raizy?"

"What?"

"Guess who's coming to visit you in a couple weeks?"

"You are."

"That's right. Grandpa Ben is coming to Israel on business! Are you going to let me have your bed?"

"Uh huh."

"What about your new teddy bear?"

Silence.

"I'm just kidding. You'll be my teddy bear."

"Oh! Are you gonna bring us presents?"

Michoel's wife coughs into her coffee on their end of the line.

"Of course I am. But it's a surprise. Now, darling, can you put your mother on for me?"

"K...one second."

Mrs. Burns takes the phone from Raizy. "Hello, Dad," she says, adjusting her purple *tichel*.

"Hello, dear. How are things doing?"

"*Baruch* Hashem, just great. Avner has a new tooth that he's putting to good use..."

"Oh, is he now? Little rascal."

"He takes after Michoel... The other day, he managed to spill over a whole box of Cheerios while my back was turned! How did he even get there, I'd like to know! I turned away for what — like, three seconds, MAYBE."

Ben smiles into the phone. "I wanted to know if you needed me to bring anything from this side of the ocean."

"Just yourself. The children are so excited! Tell me, is Mom going to be coming, too?"

"...No."

"Oh, okay. Anyway, I've got to go — I hear Moishy screaming. But can you tell Chad when you see him next at work that Michoel's been trying to reach him and Rob about something with the Foregam project?"

"No problem. Have yourself a good evening."

"You, too. Bye, Dad! Chezie, put that hammer down, or Ima is going to — "

Ben hangs up the phone and heads towards the kitchen for a snack. He smiles as he fingers the picture of his beautiful grandchildren which he always has in his pocket wallet.

"Who were you talking to?" demands a shrill voice from the living room.

"Who do you think?" Ben mutters. "Thai Chi Barney?"

"You can tell that son of yours to quit calling. We don't need to talk to him all the time."

"It was actually Raizy calling to say hello to Grandpa Ben. She wanted to speak to you also, you know."

"Did she now."

"Yes, she did."

"Hmph." But tears spring unbidden into her iced eyes. She looks over at the blown-up picture of Chad on the cover of the Time Magazine, hanging above the mantle-piece. Her pride and joy, the newest rising business magnate...

"I'm going out now," says Ben.

"Where?" she snaps, but no one answers. He must have left. She shivers into her wool shawl and looks about her cold, empty mansion with its chandeliers dripping icicles and the frigid, lackluster tiles. She is as empty as this house. No one can love her anymore, and she knows that.

Not even her husband, and it is her own stubborn fault. She pushed them all away, and now she does not know how to pull them back.

She wraps her shawl more tightly around her shoulders. She is always cold these days.

"Hey," comes a voice from the living room door. Ben stands there in his coat and shoes.

He probably tracked dirt all over the floor.

"Want to come with?" asks Ben. He holds out her coat

A chill runs up her spine. She could. It might be nice. Or does he offer out of pity? She doesn't need this.

And yet, despite this, her heart grips at her insides, tearing her apart. Somehow, she wishes she could stand up and say "yes." This isn't how she wanted it to be; this isn't how she wanted any of this to turn out. If only she had never caused reason for this, if only she could turn the clock back and right her mistakes... If only...

But she is trapped in her own cage of stubborn pride. She DIDN'T make a mistake all those years ago. It wasn't so, it couldn't be; it's too hard now to admit that it had been...that she had been wrong.

Ben is still waiting expectantly for her answer. He offers her a small smile.

Claire looks away. "No," she says.

■ ■ ■

The afternoon sky is filled with swooping doves. An orange mist of falling sun settles around the mainland as the ship pulls into the harbor.

Captain Briggs looks out over the stern of the ship as his men tie it securely to the dock.

What he once thought to be a gangplank will prove today to be nothing but a ramp to shore, and he walks down it with eyes set directly forward, a self-assured smile lighting his countenance.

On both sides of the ramp stand his men, guns held straight in the air as they salute their captain farewell. They do not understand why he wishes to retire so young, and they are sad to see him go. But his legend will always remain within their pounding and soaring hearts on those dark, cold nights alone on the ocean, when they turn to telling oft-repeated and much-extrapolated tales of high-sea adventure below deck.

Jeremy shakes his head and laughs at himself. Yeah, he wishes he was a legend. Why not? Maybe. But does it really make that much of a difference?

"Farewell, men," he whispers aloud, and then they are gone, and all he can see is four walls and the world in general, waiting for him.

■ ■ ■

Michoel stands on the balcony, *sefer* clutched to his chest, a slight breeze ruffling the loose sleeves of his shirt and brushing his face. He watches Jeremy toss a ball around in the street with his son and some neighborhood boys.

Jeremy has been living in the apartment across the hall for three months now, learning in Ohr Same'ach. He is going strong, as though trying to make up for all those lost years. They learn together Friday evenings, sharing a gemara between them because Jeremy is too comfortable after the meal to go get his own.

As he looks up at the noon sun, he smiles a small, contented sigh. Life has done him well, and he has all he needs. For he realizes now, that if you chase the sun, you cannot reach it. You just have to step outside of the shade, because the sun is waiting there patiently for you, right there, shining. Stand still, stay calm, and allow its soft rays to warm you.

Search high, search low. Look beneath the ground for gold, look above towards the planets, then look around you, and you'll find that the Torah has been there all along, and it is all you will ever need. Its warmth and its freedom...the way it all fits together, the way it fills the soul.

The way it calms the spirits and clears the mind. The way you learn and learn and still learn it, allowing its beautiful meaning to enter your life and be your life.

It's finding out that life is a whole lot more meaningful and a whole lot less complicated.

It's finding yourself.

What is Torah?

Torah is water.

Torah is life.

ACKNOWLEDGEMENTS

First and foremost, I would like to thank the Ribono Shel Olam. Without His *siyata d'Shmaya*, nothing is possible.

My dear parents: There are no words eloquent enough by which to express my gratitude for all you've done and continue to do for me.

Thank you to my siblings; my older brother for doing what brothers do best — nit-picking (how else would I know so *shtarkly* that men don't wear *taleisim* Shabbos night, all the ins and outs of *minyanim*, and the *yeshivishe hock*?); my sisters for being both the best sisters and friends I could ever ask for; and my younger brothers whose creative distractions keep me on my feet, providing me with endless laughter and reminding me of the imagination I had as a child.

Thank you to my super-cool Bubby Rivka for your love and belief in me. I love you a bushel and a peck and a hug around the neck.

Thank you to my dear friends, Gitty B., Shaindy R., Deena L., Ahuva N., Ahuva K., Perry M., and Leah H., for putting up with my bouts of busy activity and for your unconditional loyalty and devotion. You keep my spirits high; you help me believe in myself. Thank you to all those who proofread and gave their advice: Shaindy D.,Sara N., Chana F., Maidy H., Suri H., Gittle B. Gittle, and Kestie.

Thank you to my high school, Bais Yaakov of Toronto, for instilling within me a pride for my heritage. To Mrs. Weber, for setting the ideals for me to strive for and for being the best example of a true Jewish woman; to R' Silver, for showing me the *simchah* there is in being part of Klal Yisrael; and to R' Plotnick, for all the lessons he taught me about the value of Torah and how to compress my "circle of needs" in order to be happy with what I have.

I owe much *hakaras hatov* to my English teachers for training me and providing me with the skills I needed in order to write this book. Thank you to Mrs. Kakoun, Mrs. Perman, and Mrs. B. Spiro. Mrs. Spiro, this was all a dream until you showed me that my hobby could be a lot more serious than that.

Thank you to the Elzofuns in Har Nof for opening your home to me, providing me with warmth, love, ...and e-mail access. You are my safe haven.

Thank you to all my seminary friends in Mishpachas Bnos Yehudah (BYA) this year. You gave suggestions and listened to perfected versions of perfected paragraphs over and over again, even when it all sounded the same to you. Thank you for sitting and schmoozing with me as I wrote in order to keep me company, for ordering me to just sit down and finish so we could go to Geulah already, and for just being the best friends with whom to relax and let off steam. You rock my socks in Crocs!

Thank you to the staff at Israel Book Shop; to Liron Delmar, for guiding my entrance into the publishing world; to the typesetter and cover designer for turning my book into a beautiful masterpiece. To my editor, Malkie Gendelman, a huge *yasher koach* for keeping the spirit of my book alive, for your endless patience and helpful suggestions, for your gentle prodding, moving me forward to rewrite and add and perfect, for editing and transforming my story into what it is now.

Thank you to all those I may have forgotten to mention. Please know that I value all the support I was given and that your help was greatly appreciated.

M. Wiseman

About the Author

M. Wiseman wrote this book in Grade 11 as a way of occupying herself during certain classes. She is currently attending BYA seminary in Har Nof, Jerusalem. She lives with her family in Toronto, Canada and loves the snow.